A CRAZY CAT LADY AND CANINE CRUNCHIES

LARGE PRINT EDITION

ALSO BY ALEKSA BAXTER

MAGGIE MAY AND MISS FANCYPANTS MYSTERIES

A Dead Man and Doggie Delights

A Crazy Cat Lady and Canine Crunchies

A Buried Body and Barkery Bites

A Missing Mom and Mutt Munchies

A Sabotaged Celebration and Salmon Snaps

A Poisoned Past and Puppermints

***

A Fouled-Up Fourth

A Salacious Scandal and Steak Sizzlers

A Puzzling Pooch and Pumpkin Puffs

NOSY NEWFIE HOLIDAY SHORTS

Halloween at the Baker Valley Barkery & Cafe

A Housebound Holiday

A CRAZY CAT LADY

AND CANINE CRUNCHIES

A MAGGIE MAY AND MISS FANCYPANTS MYSTERY

ALEKSA BAXTER

CHAPTER 1

I was peacefully sleeping, snuggled under my comforter, all nice and warm when I heard the small little cry from the end of the bed. It was a tiny little sound, not the loud bark my Newfoundland, Miss Fancypants—Fancy for short—could've made. I mean, when you're a hundred and forty pounds you can make an awful lot of noise if you want to.

But Fancy's not like that. Our time living in an apartment when she was little had two main effects. First, she loved to wake up at the unholy hour of five-thirty every morning, rain or shine, no matter the day of the week. And, second, she was quiet but insistent.

I knew from experience that she'd make that tiny little whining sound every few seconds until I dragged myself out of bed and fed her. So even though it was my day off, it was time to get up.

I crawled out of bed and sat on the floor next to her giant dog bed. She nestled her nose against my foot and rolled on her back for a good belly rub before violently sneezing and jumping to her feet.

Time for food. (Believe it or not, that was our morning routine, sneeze and all. Not sure what it was about my foot or rolling over onto her back, but nine mornings out of ten she'd sneeze and jump to her feet within a minute of my sitting down next to her.)

I grumbled as I followed her down the hall to the kitchen. I was only thirty-six years old but after a full week of working at the barkery I felt like a little old lady. I was not used to being on my feet that much. You'd be surprised how much your body can ache after an entire day of cooking food. Standing does in fact take a lot of effort.

I'd moved to Creek, Colorado just a few weeks before to take care of my grandpa—who it turned out didn't need my help—and to open a business with my best friend Jamie. I'd known Jamie since I was little and I'd spend a month each summer with my grandparents, but she and I hadn't become best friends until we went to CU together. We bonded over a shared practicality and appreciation for people who get things done.

It had taken over a decade but we'd both finally grown tired of the corporate grind in a big city and decided to move "home" to start our own business: The Baker Valley Barkery and Café. (And no, that is not a typo. It's part bakery for dogs. Get it? Barkery? The café side serves the needs of humans. That's Jamie's side. The barkery side is for the dogs. That's my little brain child.)

And at that point, well…

Jamie makes the best cinnamon rolls in the world, so the café was doing amazing. The barkery…not so much. I was slowly building a group of steady customers like Abe and Evan at the Creek Inn, but it was slow going. If it wasn't for online sales it would have been very sad indeed.

But how many businesses are a success from day one, right? Not many. Or at least that's what I kept telling myself.

All I could do was show up each day, give it my all, and hope that things slowly trended upward.

In the meantime I finally got to work somewhere I could bring Fancy. But not that morning. It was my day off. Which meant, feed Fancy, take her for a long walk before it got too hot, and then cuddle up on the couch with a good book. My idea of a perfect day.

🐾 🐾 🐾

Of course, Fancy likes to keep me on my toes, so that's not exactly what happened.

As we set out for our morning walk, I took a deep breath of the clean mountain air. It was early summer and the sun was already up above the mountains to the east. The sky was completely clear of clouds and a gorgeous shade of blue that made me smile. There was a slight chill to the air—it was still the mountains after all—but nothing a light wind breaker couldn't handle. I'd tied my long blonde hair into a jaunty ponytail that swished back and forth with each step.

Creek was small—it had about forty houses in the town proper and maybe another couple dozen scattered through the mountains to either side—but it was mighty, too. It was the county seat and also housed the main jail, so there were a couple new buildings at the center of town in addition to the ultra-modern library at the edge of town. (A sad disappointment for me. I'd preferred when the library was in a cramped space on the third floor of the courthouse with books piled from floor to ceiling.)

We were surrounded by mountains on all sides, but not the huge towering kind you might imagine. These ones stretched just a few thousand feet above us. Easily hikeable for those who could handle the altitude.

At the end of town was a mile-or-so-wide gap where the highway led into the rest of the Baker Valley with a stream and train tracks running alongside.

I could hear a freight train passing by as we left the house, but couldn't see it from where we were. Up on the mountainside behind my grandpa's house was a large slab of rock that I'd sat on when I was a little girl, watching the trains that passed through. It didn't matter that I'd never lived in Creek full-time, this little sleepy Colorado town was where my heart had always lived.

Fancy and I walked a loop around the entire town, swinging down by the baseball park where she decided to take a bit of a breather and laid down in the grass, rolling on her back with contented grunts while I looked on in bemused annoyance. That early in the morning it was just us. Creek was never what I'd call a busy place, but before the courthouse opened it was practically dead.

That's okay. I kind of enjoyed the peace after living in DC where there was always someone watching us no matter the hour.

A Crazy Cat Lady and Canine Crunchies

We were headed back home—just in sight of Lucas Dean's house (the jerk)—when Fancy stopped in her tracks.

"Come on, Fancy. We're almost there." I tried to pull her forward, but she jumped backward instead.

Now, I am not a small woman—about five-eight, one-sixty—but when a dog the size of Fancy decides she doesn't want to go somewhere, there's not much to be done about it. And when she decides to start jumping backward a foot at a time, well...I at least am hard pressed to stay on my feet. Not to mention the danger that she'd jump right out of her collar, something she was very much trying to do.

(That happened to us once next to a very busy street and scared the living daylights out of me.)

As soon as Fancy jumped backwards the second time, I followed her and crouched down.

"What's wrong, girl? You okay?"

She was shaking like a leaf, her whole body trembling as she stared in the direction of Lucas Dean's house. Not that I thought he was the cause for her distress. I didn't like him, but he wasn't the type to send my dog into fits of terror.

"It's okay. You're fine," I soothed, speaking in that calming sing-song voice that's universally effective with kids and dogs. She burrowed her nose into my shoulder and I leaned my face against the top of her head, petting her back as I continued to calm her.

Eventually she relaxed and the trembles disappeared.

"See? It's okay. Come on now. Let's go home." I stood and tried to lead her that last crucial block towards home, but she was not having it. As soon as I started in that direction she stiffened her legs and pulled backward, all the hair bunching up around her face as her eyes bulged.

She'd go back the way we'd come, no problem. But try to move forward? Nope. Not happening.

I figured I had two choices at that point. First, I could sit on the side of the road—there wasn't a sidewalk anywhere around—and wait for her to settle down enough to move forward. Past experience told me that would take anywhere from five minutes to thirty. And that was only going to work if the cause of her distress wasn't a bear or mountain lion that decided to hang around for a while.

My second option was to try to lead her around the block and come at my grandpa's house from the other side.

(Problem with my grandpa's place is that it's at the edge of town and backed up against a mountain. So there were only two ways to get there that didn't involve climbing said mountain. One was the road we were on and the other was the road that dead-ended into that road. To get to that other road was going to require walking around a very long block.)

Since I'm not one for sitting around and hoping things will work out, I chose the second option.

Fancy was great. She walked along in front of me, doing her little Newfie sashay, happy as could be as we turned towards the highway and then walked along it. She was even great as we turned up that other road. But then she froze again.

We were within sight of my grandpa's place. It was right there. Half a block away. I thought we were gonna make it, but then she jumped backward again and sat on her butt, refusing to go one step farther.

"Come on, Fancy. Please." I held out a fistful of treats to lure her forward, but she was so scared she wouldn't even eat one. (Which for Fancy was a big, big deal. Food is Fancy's lifeblood. I remember after she was spayed the vet said she might not want to eat for a day or so, but that girl was all about her dinner that night. To the point that I was worried I might be feeding her too much so close to her surgery. She was fine, though.)

"What is wrong?" I asked, exasperated.

Of course, she couldn't tell me. She's a dog. But that doesn't keep me from making up what I think she's thinking. And from what I could tell, she was scared of something around the vicinity of my grandpa's house. Something that hadn't been there before. Which probably meant a mountain lion? Or a bear? Maybe even a coyote, although I wasn't sure they lived as high as seven thousand feet. Something was scaring her. And it was something that hadn't been there when we left the house.

I sat down cross-legged on the ground and let her sit on my lap. (No, she didn't fit. But you try telling her that when she was as upset as she was.)

I'd pretty much resigned myself to just waiting her out when a cop car turned up the street.

I buried my face in her fur. "Fancy, I swear...If that's Matt Barnes and I'm forced to talk to him because you pulled this little stunt..."

I'd done a very good job of avoiding Officer Matthew Barnes, a/k/a Officer Handsome Distraction, since he'd tried to arrest my grandpa for murder. (He hadn't wanted to. He liked my grandpa, but the evidence was pretty incriminating.) It wasn't that I disliked him. Or that I found him unappealing. He was actually mighty fine looking, especially in a cop's uniform—the epitome of tall, dark, and handsome and with blue eyes to boot.

It was just that I had better things to do with my time than pine after some hot guy. I was starting a new business. And taking care of Fancy. And my grandpa. And I'd just moved there. Last thing I needed was to get all caught up with someone.

Better to avoid him than to let myself get distracted at such a crucial time in my life.

(Of course, both Jamie and my grandpa would point out that I always thought it was a crucial time to avoid distraction. Whatever. I had plans, so sue me.)

CHAPTER 2

The car pulled up next to us and the driver rolled the window down. Sure enough. It was Matt.

"Taking a little break?" He grinned down at us.

Fancy leapt to her feet, wagging her tail in giddy excitement at the sound of his voice. She's such a traitor. I swear, she loves every man more than she loves me, although Matt is a particular favorite. Her tail slapped me in the face a few times before I managed to stand up myself.

I walked over to the car and before I could stop her, Fancy had jumped up and shoved her head through the window and licked his face. Rather than recoil in disgust like most people would, he just laughed and rubbed at her ears until she was groaning in pleasure.

"How's my girl?" he asked, kissing her on the nose.

"If something ever happens to me, at least I know she'll have a good home," I muttered.

He laughed. "Not me. Your grandpa would never let her go."

It was probably true. My grandpa tried to play it cool when it came to Fancy, but it was pretty clear he adored her as much as she adored him.

"Good point."

"So? You guys were just taking a break on the side of the road?"

(It wasn't unheard of for me to do that. When we still lived in an apartment and Fancy was a puppy she'd want to stay outside forever and so I'd sit on the sidewalk while she sat on the grass and watched the world go by. I'm sure people thought I was nuts, especially in Crystal City. And **especially** when I threw leaves for her to catch. That's okay. I kind of am.)

A Crazy Cat Lady and Canine Crunchies

I told him about my failed attempts to lead Fancy home. "I'm kind of outta options at this point. So I figured we'd sit here until she calmed down enough to make it the last little bit."

"That might take a while depending on what's spooking her."

"I know. But what other choice do I have?"

"You could let me give you a ride."

I shoved my immediate thought about that little comment aside and nodded. "That could work."

And it did. At first. Fancy jumped into the back of the car without any hesitation whatsoever. (It was weird back there. You'd think they'd have upholstered seats, but they don't. It's this strange hard plastic. I guess that makes it easier to clean up whatever fluids people might bring with them. I know. Ew. But when people are drunk or in fights, I'm sure they're not exactly clean by the time the cops show up.)

I sat next to her, but she still slid around a bit as we drove to my grandpa's house. At least it wasn't far; just half a block. Where we had the real problem was when it came time to get out of the car.

Fancy was not having it. And she made her opinion known with a lot of loud barking at both of us. Not her angry bark. This was her "why would you do this horrible thing to me?" bark that's loud and whiny all at the same time.

"Fancy! Matt needs to get to work. Get out of that car right now."

She, of course, ignored me. That's the problem with governing through bribery. When your dog is too upset to be bribed, it all falls apart.

Finally, Matt just grabbed her by the collar and dragged her out of the car. With that crazy plastic all over the place she scrambled to resist him, but couldn't. He didn't hurt her, but it surprised me nonetheless. I would've never even considered doing that.

As soon as Fancy's feet touched the ground and she realized she no longer had access to the safety of the car, she ducked her head down, hunched her shoulders, and raced for the front door. I chased after her, kind of glad for the excuse to get away from Officer Handsome.

"Thank you," I shouted back at him as I caught up with Fancy at the front door.

"You're welcome. I'd say you owe me a dinner for that one."

I pretended not to hear him. Matt is a horrible cook, at least from what he's said, but the last thing I needed was for him to come over for dinner.

My grandpa stepped outside as I let Fancy in. He was wearing his normal outfit of a short-sleeved plaid shirt over a plain white t-shirt and faded Levi's. For a man of eighty-two he looks at least a decade younger if not more, probably thanks to the fact that his hair is just a faded brown instead of white or gray. "You say something about dinner, Matt?"

I ducked inside as he walked towards Matt's car, knowing there was no point in trying to stop him. I wondered where Fancy had gone to. She'd disappeared around the corner as soon as I set her free, but I didn't know where she'd gone from there.

Finally, I found her. She was curled up in the far corner of my bedroom—a place she never goes during the day—her big amber eyes staring up at me.

I sat down next to her, careful not to sit too close because then she'd just run away. "It's okay, kiddo. You're safe now." I pet her soft black head and gave her a little kiss between the eyes. She stared up at me, her eyes full of love and trust.

I sighed. "You know I love you, but you did not do me any favors just now."

Dogs and men...I tell ya.

CHAPTER 3

The next day at the barkery started off well. I actually had a few customers and my newest treat—Canine Crunchies—seemed to be a hit with its target audience. I'd needed some sort of treat that would hold up well and was large enough that I could offer it to unknown dogs without the risk of losing a finger. So far, so good.

But then Janice Fletcher walked in the door. Janice was an older woman who never got the memo that it's bad for the environment to use that much hairspray. And that mustard-colored polyester slacks went out of style at least a few decades ago.

Trailing behind her was her best friend, Patsy Blackstone, who had the unfortunate habit of trying to match her clothes to her hair color. Seeing as her hair was some unfortunate shade of orange that was probably supposed to be red, it was not a good look.

I could've forgiven their unfortunate sartorial choices. (See eleventh grade English teacher, I knew someday I'd make that worthless vocabulary word work for me.) A customer is a customer after all, and I certainly needed more of them.

But Janice came in with a carrycase in hand—the plastic kind you see people use to take their pets on a plane. Again, not necessarily a problem. We were a bakery for dogs after all.

It was when she headed right for the center table with a defiant glare in my direction, set the case on the table, and opened it up that the trouble began. She pulled a large, furry white cat out while it meowed in protest at being taken from its comfortable bed. I immediately sneezed because I am very, very allergic to cats, especially big, fluffy white ones.

A Crazy Cat Lady and Canine Crunchies

"Janice." I smiled as politely as I could. "This is a **dog** bakery. Cats aren't allowed. It says it right there on the door."

She set the cat on the table and let go of him. (Or her, who can tell.) "My Pookums has as much right to be here as any dog."

"Well, no. Actually that's not true." I moved closer, not wanting to antagonize her, but also wanting to keep that cat away from the dog treat counter. I was just glad no one was there other than Fancy who was snoring away in her cubby.

(If you'll recall the café and barkery is set up with two separate sides that have an area to pass through right by the back counter. On the barkery side there are some smaller nooks along the far wall for dogs that need to be left for a minute or two as well as well-spaced tables throughout the rest of the space that allow plenty of room for canine companions to join their owners while at the same time minimizing the possibility of any fights or someone tripping over a paw. Fancy has her very own cubby in the back corner with an extra-large dog bed where she spends most of the day snoring away. In the area between the café counter and the barkery counter there's also a little shop area with touristy items like mugs with our logo on them and pre-packaged dog treats. On the other side of that is the café counter.)

Janice stood up straighter, a wicked gleam in her eye. "Are you saying that cats aren't allowed here?"

"Yes. I am."

Pookums chose that moment to jump down and run across the floor towards the bright and shiny items on sale in the touristy area. Within seconds he'd managed to swat down a handful of keychains and knock a mug to the floor where it shattered loudly, forcing Fancy to jump to her feet and bark in fright.

"Jamie," I shouted. "I need your help. Now!" I glared at Janice. "**That** is why cats are not allowed in here. If you can't keep control of your pet, you can't be in here."

"A dog would do the same thing," Janice spat back at me.

"Well none has. We have a strict leash rule here. You're paying for that mug, by the way." I turned to quiet Fancy.

"I am not. How can you run an establishment like this and expect to leave breakable goods just lying around like that? It's not my fault the mug broke."

I waved a treat under Fancy's nose, but she'd spotted the cat and was not in the mood to quiet down. "Get your frickin' cat and get out of here," I hissed at Janice

(I know. Not the best example of customer service. And especially not in a small town and with a witness who was on the other person's side. But honestly...)

Jamie scooped Pookums up and smiled at both of us. He batted at her brunette braid as she cooed at him and walked towards Janice. "Here. Let me help you put him back in his case," she said, doing so before anyone could stop her.

"You can't expect me to keep Pookums locked up the whole time I'm here," Janice huffed.

I glared at her. "Actually, I don't. I expect you to take him home. Now."

I sneezed. Crazy cat lady and her frickin' white-haired ball of allergies. If that cat was around for much longer I was going to need a shower or have to risk my throat swelling shut.

🐾 🐾 🐾

Now, before we continue, I feel I need to say a few things because you may be a cat lover and I don't want you to get the wrong idea here. I have nothing against cat lovers in general. I think anyone who can love any animal, be it a dog, cat, or rhinoceros, is a good person.

And as a crazy dog lady myself I understand how someone can love their cat to the point of dressing it in costumes and talking to it in a baby voice. Only reason I don't do that with Fancy is she'd probably sit on me the first time I tried to put her in some weird outfit.

So I have nothing against cat people. Or cats for that matter. (Other than the fact that I am insanely allergic to them and that, somehow psychically knowing this, they all try to rub up against my legs or sit on my face. True story: I once woke up to find my friend's kitten curled in a little ball on my throat.)

So when I call her a crazy cat lady it has nothing to do with any other cat owner on this planet. I just wanted Janice Fletcher and her sneeze-inducing feline friend to leave.

🐾 🐾 🐾

"This isn't fair." Janice glared at me as Patsy crowded up behind her nodding in agreement.

"Life isn't fair. Now please leave my establishment. Do not make me call the cops." I'd finally gotten Fancy calmed down by throwing a handful of canine crunchies into her cubby, so walked back to Janice, ready to throw her out on her ear if I had to.

"The cops!" Janice's face turned a violent shade of red. "You wouldn't dare!"

I opened my mouth to say I would, too, but Jamie gently pushed me backward and stepped between us. "Ms. Fletcher, there really are a number of reasons we can't have cats here in the barkery. You have to see that. It's just not safe. And not hygienic to have a cat, or any animal really, running loose in a food establishment."

She handed the carrier to Ms. Fletcher and gently guided her towards the door, Patsy trailing along uncertainly behind them.

"I'm sorry we couldn't accommodate you and your cat." Jamie held the door open for them, smiling in such a way that she was impossible to refuse. "But if you ladies want to come back sometime **without** the cat, I'd be more than happy to give you each a free cinnamon roll."

Before they even knew what was happening, Janice, Patsy, and Pookums were outside and Jamie was closing the door in their face, calmly but firmly.

(Somedays I wish I were her. I'm a little too fiery to pull something like that off as you might have noticed.)

A Crazy Cat Lady and Canine Crunchies

"Well." She pretended to dust her hands off. "Hopefully that's the last of that."

"Hopefully. Thanks for the assist." I turned to Fancy. "And, you, young lady...You can't bark at customers like that."

Jamie laughed and patted me on the shoulder. "I'd say that's the pot calling the kettle black, wouldn't you?"

"Hey!"

"It's true. You also can't be barking at customers. Not if you want us to be open six months from now."

"I know, but...Seriously. She was looking for a fight."

"Doesn't mean you needed to give her one."

Jamie was right, but I didn't have to like it.

CHAPTER 4

At least one good thing happened that day, even if it came with an unpleasant surprise.

Around one o'clock the barkery door chimed and I looked up to see who was there. The first person through the door was an attractive woman who was probably slightly older than I am. She wore slim slacks, a brightly colored top, and a tasteful, but expensive amount of jewelry. (All except her wedding ring which was visible from across the room.) Her pale blonde hair and skin told me she was probably from or descended from a long line of people from Sweden, Norway, Iceland, Germany, etc.

A Crazy Cat Lady and Canine Crunchies

She also had a dog with her. (Well, two, but we'll get to that in a moment.)

The first dog, the real one, was an Irish wolfhound. He was tall—his head easily reached above her waist—but slim and wiry. I figured he and Fancy were about the same height but she probably had at least twenty pounds on him, if not more. Not that I thought she'd win in a fight. He looked nice enough, but there was a coiled energy to him that made me very glad his owner seemed to be in such firm control of him.

Holding the door open for this intriguing pair of guests was none other than Lucas Dean—a man who should've been in jail if the world were in any way fair. (That would be the second dog I mentioned above.) He grinned at me from behind the woman with that cock-sure smile of his that charmed everyone but me.

Don't get me wrong, I could acknowledge that Luke was a good-looking man in a "convince you to sneak out of your house at midnight and spend a few hours in the bed of his truck" sort of way. I just knew he was a lying, cheating jerk, too. And one that had broken Jamie's heart at least a half dozen times over the years. She kept going back to him, which was the worst of it.

For a smart woman, she was horrible at choosing men.

I gritted my teeth and forced a smile, focusing my attention on the woman. Luke I'd deal with later. He knew darned well he wasn't supposed to set foot in the barkery or the café ever again.

"Welcome to the Baker Valley Barkery and Café," I said. "May I?" I gestured towards the dog as I came around the counter with a canine crunchy in hand.

"Yes. Hans loves a good treat." The woman barked some command in what sounded like German and Hans immediately sat. (I bet **she** wouldn't have had a problem getting Fancy to go home...)

"Nice to meet you, Hans." I held my empty hand out to him to smell and then offered him the treat. He

A Crazy Cat Lady and Canine Crunchies

took it with what I can only call an extreme amount of class.

"Hi. I'm Maggie." I held out my hand to his owner.

The woman took it with a surprisingly firm grip. I was expecting some sort of limp squeeze and release, but she shook hands like a businesswoman. "Greta VanVeldenstein. I have moved here but construction continues on my home. Lucas says this is an excellent place to bring Hans for a break from the noise. He gave me samples of your treats. Hans likes them very much." Her accent was slightly Germanic, but not terribly strong.

"Oh, wonderful. Welcome. I'm sure you'll love it here. Baker Valley is certainly one of my favorite places in the world. May I ask? Where are you originally from?"

"Ah, the accent, yes? Germany. Although I have not been back since the death of my second husband." She smoothed a hand through her hair and turned towards the café side. "Lucas tells me you also have coffee and food?"

Lucas stepped forward. "I'll get something for you, Mrs. VanVeldenstein. Why don't you and Hans make yourselves comfortable. A soup and panini with a black coffee, perhaps?"

She nodded. "Yes. Perfect. Thank you."

Lucas shot me a grin as he dashed towards the café side. (And Jamie.) I wanted to grab him by the ear, drag him to the door, and throw him out, but I couldn't in front of my newest customer and he knew it.

I smiled at Greta. "Well, as you can see, it's pretty quiet right now. So feel free to choose any table you want and let me know if there's anything else I can do for you."

"Will you join me? For lunch? I have a book, but I prefer company over a meal."

"Um, sure. I can do that." I glanced towards where Lucas was leaning against the counter making Jamie laugh.

"He will not join us. I promise."

I winced. "That obvious, am I?"

A Crazy Cat Lady and Canine Crunchies

She shrugged one shoulder. "You will tell me why sometime. But not today. I do not think he is an ex?"

"Oh no. Not mine at least."

She looked more carefully towards the counter. "Ah, yes. I see now. Your friend. The other owner?"

I nodded.

"Then she must join us, too. And Lucas will go back to work."

"I like that plan. Just give me a moment to get the rest of the food arranged and we'll be back to join you."

As I raced to break up Luke and Jamie, and also prepare myself some soup and panini, Greta chose the table in the center of the picture window, Hans settling down comfortably at her feet. Despite her unfortunate association with Lucas Dean, I was giddy with excitement.

I had my first real customer!

CHAPTER 5

Greta turned out to be delightful. It was clear from a few things she said here or there that she was not only wealthy but obscenely rich. I didn't mind, though, because she didn't look down her nose at either of us. She was just sweet and charming. A little odd, I'll give you that. She told us Hans was named for one of her husbands, but she wasn't quite sure which one he'd been. Probably number five or six; definitely not numbers one through four.

"How many times have you been married?" I asked her, laughing.

"It is so hard to remember. Some were very short. And some I think I married but maybe I did not. I believe Friedrich, my current husband, is number nine. Or ten? Maybe number eleven."

Jamie laughed. "Why so many?"

She shrugged a shoulder. "This is a good question. The first marriage was for love. I was young. He was handsome. That was all it took. The second marriage was for money. I was young. I was beautiful. He was not. But he was kind. And wealthy. And then...I do not know. I thought marriage was what you do, yes? Now? Perhaps not." She looked back and forth between us. "And you? You have been married, yes?"

"No." I shook my head in horror. "I don't have time for any of that."

Greta laughed. "You say this because you have not been married. The right husband can be very good for a woman." She narrowed her eyes at me. "But it is best that the first husband be for money. That is the mistake I made when young."

I didn't even know what to say to that. "Ah..."

"Oh, you think you marry for love?" She laughed. "This will disappoint you. He will be human. And you will be sad. Money is better. I will find you someone. My husband has a friend. He would make a good first husband. He is very old and very rich."

I shook my head in horror. "Really, it's..."

"No, no, no. I insist." She turned to Jamie. "And you, Jamie? Have you been married?"

"No." Jamie looked away.

"But you would like to be."

"Um, yeah, I think so." She fiddled with her coffee spoon in a very un-Jamie-like way.

I stared at her. Since when? Please tell me she wasn't thinking of marrying Lucas Dean.

Greta nodded. "Then I will find you a rich man, too."

Jamie started to open her mouth to object, but Greta patted her hand. "This Lucas is a fun man, yes? But he is not a man you marry."

"I don't know about that. I mean he's..."

"No. Listen to me. I have been married many, many times. I know what makes a good husband and Lucas...No. He does not." She patted Jamie's hand again. "We will find you a good husband. I think you would not want to be a mistress?"

I almost spit out my Coke at that one. "No, Greta. Neither of us would like to be a mistress."

She shrugged and sat back. "It would be easier if you would. More choices. But I understand. I too am not a good mistress."

We were saved from the rest of that conversation by the jangle of the door as someone came in on the café side. "Be right there," Jamie called as she hustled away more quickly than was absolutely necessary.

I gathered up the dishes from lunch. "I should probably get back to work myself. But I really hope you'll come back."

"I will. The construction in my home is very loud. Hans and I need a break. May we stay?"

"Of course. Stay as long as you'd like." I winced as I glanced around at all the empty tables. "Not like we're hurting for space right now."

"It is a nice place you have here, Maggie. Give it time."

"Thank you."

I walked away buoyed by the thought of a new customer and perhaps a new friend. No doubt, Greta was half off her rocker, but sometimes those are the best sorts of friends to have.

🐾 🐾 🐾

And Greta was true to her word. She was there at one o'clock every day for the rest of the week, with her laptop or her book to entertain her, and usually stayed until we closed at four. Hans just slept at her feet the whole time, ten times more well-behaved than Fancy. She's good—don't get me wrong—but Fancy does need to be let into the dog run out back every couple of hours and will definitely make it known when that needs to happen.

Things were finally looking up. I had my first regular customer, some of the local businesses were stocking my dog treats for their customers to buy, and online sales had picked up, too. I was happy.

A Crazy Cat Lady and Canine Crunchies

Until Janice Fletcher returned.

🐾 🐾 🐾

Fortunately, Jamie was able to catch me before I left the house. (She's always in earlier because she does all the baking in the morning.)

"Hey, Jamie, what's up?" I asked as I pulled on my second tennis shoe, my phone cradled between my ear and shoulder.

"You better leave Fancy at home today."

"What? Why?" I glanced at Fancy who was already standing by the door staring at her leash and collar like they might run away and escape if she didn't keep a good eye on them.

"Janice Fletcher is back. And she's not alone."

"You're not even open yet. What's she doing?"

"She's gathered a little group of friends from what I can tell. And they all have signs." She sighed. "I think she's going to picket us."

"Picket? What for?"

"Not allowing her cat, I'd assume."

"Oh that's ridiculous."

My grandpa raised an eyebrow as he walked past me headed for the kitchen and his first cup of coffee. He's not much of a talker until he's had his morning caffeine.

Jamie sighed again. "Ridiculous or not, I think it's best not to bring Fancy through this mess. All we need is for someone to crowd too close and she barks at them and then it's all over the news. Janice's nephew, Peter Nielsen, runs the local paper, remember? I'm sure he'll be here, too, before long."

"That twerp is her nephew?" (I didn't like him much. I'd tried to get him to cover our grand opening and he'd made some nasty comment to me about how a two-bit café that'd be closed in less than a year wasn't news.)

"Yep. So leave Fancy at home."

"Okay. Will do." I hung up and looked to Fancy. She'd lain down in front of the door, staring at me. She may not be able to talk, but that girl can figure things out better than most people.

"Fancy..."

She didn't move, just stared at me with those big amber eyes of hers.

"I'm going to have to leave you at home today. But you get to hang out with Grandpa. You'll like that won't you?"

She harrumphed and laid her head on her paws.

"I can't do anything about this, Fancy. So don't look at me that way. Now move. I need to get your bed from the van."

She scrambled to her feet as I opened the door, but then tried to go outside with me when I opened it. I barely blocked her with my leg. "I'm sorry, Fancy. You have to stay behind."

I snuck past her and closed the door firmly behind me, feeling like the most horrible human being on the planet. But if Jamie was right about what Janice Fletcher had planned, then I really did need to leave Fancy at home. For her sake. Plus, she loved my grandpa. She might be acting all hurt and disappointed now, but she'd probably forget all about me once I was gone. Or so I told myself.

(Just like I'd told myself how much she loved daycare when I was living in DC. She did, but it was no substitute for time in the park with me.)

I lugged the extra-large dog bed back to the house.

"What's that for?" my grandpa muttered, taking a long sip of his coffee. "That dog has enough dog beds already."

I handed him the morning paper that I'd snagged while I was outside. "It's for your workroom."

I dragged the bed down the hall and wedged it into the far corner of the room before he could object. He loves to work on miniatures even though his hands tremble so bad some days it takes him five minutes to place one little piece. And I figured if Fancy was going to be home with him all day she'd want a comfy spot to keep him company while he worked.

"What do you mean, it's for my workroom?" he asked when I returned.

I flashed him my best smile. "Fancy has to stay here today."

"Doesn't mean she needs a bed in my workroom."

"Well she's going to want to stay close to you. And lying on the floor can hurt her joints."

"She has a bed in the living room. She has a bed in your room. She has a bed in my room. She has a bed in the office. And now you think she needs a bed in my workroom, too?"

"I don't have time to argue about this. I'm running late. Fancy needs to stay here today. Please look after her. And please, let the bed stay?"

He muttered something under his breath before taking a long sip of his coffee, but at least he didn't continue the argument.

I turned to Fancy who was now leaning against the wall watching me. "I'm sorry, girl. I have to go. You have to stay here."

She ran to the door and looked back at me, eyes wide.

"No. You have to stay here."

She sank onto her haunches, every line of her body full of hurt and rejection.

I closed my eyes for a moment and took a deep breath. Disappointing a dog is never easy.

Fortunately, Fancy is easily distracted. I ran into the kitchen and grabbed her a doggie ice cream from the freezer. She immediately perked up when she saw what I had in my hand.

"I will have you know that it is way too early in the day for you to be eating something like this," I told her.

She didn't care. I'm not even sure she was hearing what I said at that point. All of her attention was focused on the ice cream treat in my hand.

"Be good for Grandpa. I'll be home in...ten hours." (I knew that wouldn't mean anything to her. She's actually pretty good at telling time, but anything past about five hours is just "a long frickin' time" in Fancyworld.)

I handed her the container and she immediately raced out back to eat her ice cream while I made a quick exit. "Love you, Grandpa."

"Love you, too."

CHAPTER 6

I drove towards the barkery wondering just how bad this little protest demonstration was going to be. I mean, how many crazy cat ladies can one town have? One? Two? Three at most, I'd think.

Turns out the answer was ten. Which seriously surprised me. Who knew there were ten women in the Baker Valley who were so passionate about bringing their cats out to lunch with them that they'd gather to protest our store at seven in the morning?

But there they were. Janice was brandishing a hand-made sign that read "Cats Need Love Too" with little cat paw prints painted on it. Next to her Patsy Blackstone had a sign that read "Cat Hater!" written in a color that looked very much like fresh blood but clearly was not since it was still bright, bright red. The other signs were just as absurd. And the other women looked to have dressed themselves out of the same out-of-date, over-the-top fashion magazine as Janice and Patsy.

Wow. Just...wow.

As I approached the front of the store they converged on me, waving their signs and shouting out little phrases about what a horrible, cat-hating person I was. I'll give them this, they were all in with their protest. But I am not a morning person at the best of times. And when you make me leave my dog at home and then surround me with bad perfume and loud shouting, well, you get the worst of me.

"Back off!" I snapped.

(There may have been two more words in the middle of that sentence, but let's just go with back off for the sake of politeness.)

They gasped and stared at me in horror, moving like some sort of twisted version of the Stepford Brides.

"Did you hear what she said?" one of the ladies said to another.

This after waving a sign in my face and shouting at me?

I glared them down. "Leave now or I'm calling the cops."

"We have every right to protest an unfair establishment." Janice planted herself directly in front of me, the ladies arraying themselves behind her.

"You may in fact have every right to protest the fact that we don't allow cats. But you do not have the right to threaten me or anyone else who wants to enter my establishment. So back off."

(Once more, there might have been a couple extra words thrown in there.)

Janice stepped closer. "Or what?"

Fortunately for me, I heard the little chirp of a cop car trying to clear a crowd and the sound of tires on gravel behind me. The cavalry had arrived.

A Crazy Cat Lady and Canine Crunchies

The ladies all backed up an extra step, but they didn't disperse. I was tempted to turn around and see who it might be, but Janice and I were locked in the midst of an intense staredown and I wasn't going to be the one to blink first.

She needed to know who she was dealing with.

I heard the car door slam and the sound of the cop's feet on the pavement as he approached. "What seems to be the problem here?" he asked.

I winced. It was Officer Clark—the man who'd dragged my eighty-two-year-old grandpa out of his home in handcuffs and who would probably arrest him again given half the chance.

"Officer Clark. These women are disrupting my business."

He crossed his arms and pursed his lips, looking back and forth between the women and the front of our store.

Janice turned to him. "We have every right to protest."

I took a deep breath. Being angry and irrational wasn't going to help any. "I realize that they probably do have the right to protest, but I would ask that they do so somewhere that doesn't threaten or intimidate our customers."

He smirked at me. "They're little old ladies. They're not threatening anyone."

"Do not call me a little old lady."

I thought for a second Janice was going to whap him with her sign, but she stopped herself just in time.

"See?" I said. "When I arrived all ten of them converged on me. I'd really appreciate it if you could keep them from doing that to my customers."

I was pretty sure he was going to ignore me and let them continue their protests. And then I didn't know what I was going to do. If the cops won't help you, what other options do you have?

But another cop car pulled into the parking lot. It was Matt. I'd never been so happy to see him in my life. (Not that I let myself feel that for more than a split second, because...reasons.)

He stepped out of his car with a nod and smile for all of the ladies.

"Hi, Officer Barnes," one of the ladies called. "You never have said whether you'd like to come over for Sunday dinner. My niece would love to meet you."

"I'm sure she would, Ms. Highsmith, but I'm still pretty tied up with taking care of my father's house and starting the new job and all."

Liar. I was pretty sure he spent most of his free time crashed out on his couch watching TV.

"What seems to be the problem," he asked, joining us and looking pointedly at Officer Clark.

"These ladies are protesting the fact that the owners of this establishment won't allow cats."

"They swarmed me when I arrived," I added.

Officer Clark glared at me, but I didn't care. It was true.

"Janice," Matt turned his charming smile her way. "We've been through this before. You can't obstruct a business this way."

She glared at him, but didn't answer.

He turned and scanned the parking lot. "You and your ladies can protest, but you will have to do it over there." He pointed to a grassy area at the far end of the parking lot, at least a hundred feet from the entrance. "No shouting at customers either, even if they park right by you."

"No one will see us over there."

"They'll see you just fine, Janice. Look, Peter Nielsen just pulled in. I'm sure you'll be on the front page of the paper tomorrow. If that doesn't make your point for you, I don't know what will. Now go."

"Before he can take his pictures?"

"Yes. Now."

Janice looked like she was going to argue her point further, but when Matt wants to be intimidating he's very good at it. She stormed away in a huff, her ladies following after like a gaggle of geese.

Jamie came out as soon as they started to walk away, a coffee in each hand. "Can I offer you gentlemen a drink?"

Officer Clark turned to snarl at her, but stopped himself when he saw the attractive woman holding a cup of coffee for him. Jamie flashed him a dimpled smile with a head tilt.

I felt ill. Not Officer Clark, please. I'd rather she kept seeing Lucas Dean.

"Officer Barnes?" She held out the other cup of coffee.

"Best not. Wouldn't want to be seen playing favorites." He winked at me before returning to his patrol car.

Whatever that was about.

"Well, then. Now that that's over." I rushed into the barkery as fast as I could. I was not going to think about Matthew Barnes one moment longer than I had to.

(Even though I was extremely grateful he'd saved us from the cadre of crazy cat ladies outside.)

🐾 🐾 🐾

The rest of the day was fairly uneventful although I was not amused by the pictures and article that Peter Nielsen posted to his website for the noon edition of the **Baker Valley Gazette**. It accused us of being elitist snobs from the big city who didn't want the scummy locals messing up our place. The fact that the protest was about cats was barely even mentioned.

I had to give the man credit. He knew how to stir up controversy.

We spent the afternoon dealing with angry locals who stormed into the store to tell us they had as much of a right to frequent our establishment as some hoity-toity tourist. (Having poor Greta sitting in the front window of the barkery certainly didn't help, but I didn't have the heart to tell her to leave. She was my only regular customer after all.)

Jamie handled it with aplomb. Each time someone stormed through the door Jamie greeted them with a big smile, a coffee, and a cinnamon roll. On the house. By three o'clock we were getting freebie seekers who could barely pretend to be angry, but she treated them all the same.

A Crazy Cat Lady and Canine Crunchies

Chalk it up as a business expense. Like I've said before, Jamie makes the best cinnamon rolls in the world. By the end of the day, thanks to Janice Fletcher, everyone in the county knew it.

Victory snatched from the jaws of defeat. Take that, Janice.

🐾 🐾 🐾

Even though the day had turned out well, I'd missed Fancy. She may spend most of every day snoring in her cubby, but it's still nice to have her around. So when I returned home I was more than happy to sit down on the floor and let her crawl all over me and lick my face for a good five minutes.

My grandpa said she'd spent most of the day lying five feet from the door waiting for me to come home. Poor girl. Seems she'd missed me as much as I'd missed her. Too bad I was going to have to leave her at home another day. No telling what Janice was going to pull next.

CHAPTER 7

You're probably wondering at this point why I'm telling you all of this and no one's shown up dead yet. Don't worry, it's coming. But I felt I needed to get all the pieces in place first so you'd understand how it was I ended up in jail for murder.

Yep, me.

But first...

After Janice's failed attempt to boycott our business things actually settled down for a few days. Other than a nice little bump in sales of cinnamon rolls, it was like it had never happened. We actually had to hire in some temporary counter staff so Jamie could spend more time in the kitchen preparing four-packs of cinnamon rolls that we sold throughout the day. It was beautiful.

A Crazy Cat Lady and Canine Crunchies

To tell you the truth, I almost wanted to kiss Janice and Peter Nielsen for their brilliance in driving so many new customers our way.

I should've known it wouldn't last.

Janice and Patsy barged through the barkery door at two o'clock one afternoon, cat carriers in hand. That's right. Carriers plural. Each of them had one.

I took a deep, deep breath. Jamie was in the back and I knew the elderly woman working the café counter would be no help in banishing these women for once and for all.

"Janice. Please leave my store. I have told you repeatedly that cats are not allowed here."

I glanced towards Greta who'd put down her book and was watching us with interest. Hans was still his usual calm and collected self, but there was no doubt he was focused on the two carriers and what they might contain.

I did not need this. If they let those cats out and Hans wasn't good around cats...

Janice shoved a piece of paper in my face. "It doesn't matter what you want. You can't make me leave. Pookums has every right to be here. I need him."

I scanned the paper. "Are you serious?"

She stood up straighter. "Of course I am."

"You had Pookums declared an emotional support cat?"

"Yes."

I glanced at the date. "You only got this letter yesterday."

"I was just making official what's always been true. I need my Pookums with me."

I pressed my lips together, hard.

CHAPTER 8

Yet again, I feel I have to take a moment and explain something here. I have nothing against emotional support animals. I've met a number of wonderful support animals over the years—ones that allowed people with anxiety to experience the world and ones that could detect potential seizures. I am all for emotional support animals. And if someone had walked into my store with a cat as a legitimate emotional support animal, I would've made it work.

I assume they would've kept that cat close, though. And that they would've understood that taking a cat into a dog barkery wasn't going to be the best idea. But if they'd insisted on being there, I would've respected that.

But this?

This was not legitimate. And Janice Fletcher knew that as well as I did. Which is why I went from calm to trembling with rage in about ten seconds. Not only was this woman trying everything she could to mess with my business but she was taking advantage of something that should be respected.

🐾 🐾 🐾

"Jamie," I shouted.

She came out of the kitchen, her smock covered in baking flour and a small smudge on the side of her nose. "What? What's wrong?"

"You need to deal with this." I shoved the letter into her hands, glared at Janice and Patsy for a long moment, and then retreated to the barkery counter. I literally felt like breaking something in that moment, but I knew I couldn't. Not without making things worse.

As I stood there I fantasized about taking up a sport like taekwondo that would let me break boards. I could keep a stack out in the dog run and go back there and shatter them into little pieces whenever I needed a release. (It's possible customer service is not exactly my forte.)

I spent the next few minutes while Jamie dealt with Janice Fletcher and Patsy Blackstone, mentally breaking boards. Finally, Jamie had it settled. "Please follow me."

She turned towards the café side.

"Where are you taking us?" Janice demanded.

"I appreciate that you have an emotional support animal, but in the interest of safety and health, I have to ask that you come sit on the café side away from any dogs. You'll receive the same level of service and have the same menu of options to order from, but I can't let you sit on this side."

"I'll sue you."

Jamie stared her down. "For what? We're letting you stay here."

"It's discrimination."

"No. It's not. Now, please. Follow me." There was steel behind her words.

Janice and Patsy reluctantly followed her to the other side of the store, glaring back at me with each step. I knew this wasn't over. I knew they'd be back, demanding to sit on the barkery side. I didn't know why, but that woman had it in for me.

I grabbed a cleaning rag and wiped down all of the tables even though they were already clean.

Greta called me over. "What is this that happened just now?"

I explained to her about the cat issue and how now Janice had found a way around my ban by having her cat declared an emotional support animal. Greta found the whole concept very confusing but admitted she had heard some of the same news stories I had about emotional support peacocks and fish.

She shook her head. "This woman, she is wrong. She must be dealt with."

"Agreed. I'm just not sure how."

CHAPTER 9

About twenty minutes later Jamie came to join us. "They're gone. Thankfully. I managed to convince them to keep the cats in their carriers this time, but that won't work next time."

"You're a saint, Jamie. I was ready to kill that woman."

"I know." She chuckled. "Your face was very, very red when I came over."

"So what do we do now?"

"Already done." She waved her phone at me. "I took a copy of the letters and called Mason Maxwell. He'll be by in an hour or so."

"Mason Maxwell? Really?"

He was an amazing attorney. The best in the county. But he also intimidated the heck out of me and was not cheap. I should know. He'd helped us out with my grandpa's little murder charge.

"He's the best. Aaand...It turns out his family and Janice's hate each other."

"I didn't realize there was a big Maxwell contingent in Baker Valley. Or Fletcher for that matter."

"Oh, Mason Maxwell is a Mason. When his mother married out of the family, she gave him Mason as a first name so he'd still carry the family legacy."

"You mean Mason as in Masonville, the town? One of the founding families of the valley?"

"Yep. And Janice Fletcher was a Baker before she got married. One of the other founding families of the valley. They've hated each other since day one."

"This Mason, he is rich?" Greta asked. "And single?"

We both looked at her. What did that have to do with anything?

"I have no idea, Greta," I said. She was certainly an odd one at times.

A Crazy Cat Lady and Canine Crunchies

"Why don't you ask him when he gets here," Jamie suggested, trying not to smile. She pushed herself to her feet. "In the meantime, I'm going to finish up this last batch of cinnamon rolls for the day." She glanced towards the kitchen. "Who knew I'd come to hate baking cinnamon rolls as much as I did drafting analysis reports?"

"I can do some of the baking tomorrow if you want," I offered.

"I might just take you up on that."

Jamie was a genius in the kitchen, but I could hold my own when I wanted to, especially if I was working from one of her recipes. I put that aside for the time being, though. Mason Maxwell was headed our way and for some reason I felt that warranted a tidying up binge. He wasn't exactly condescending, but he was very clearly a man with standards that most people didn't meet.

If he was going to be our attorney in this, I wanted to make the best impression possible.

🐾 🐾 🐾

Mason Maxwell walked through the door exactly an hour later. With his salt and pepper hair and country club attire (nice slacks and a polo shirt this time), he looked very out of place in our cutesy kitschy little café. I felt like he weighed and judged the entire place with that steely gaze of his.

Greta was still there and she watched him with a studied bemusement. Given the amount of money she had some mere millionaire wasn't going to phase her one bit.

"Mr. Maxwell," I said. "Thank you for coming out on such short notice."

"It is the nature of my business," he replied. "How is your grandfather?"

"He's well, thank you. No more cops showing up to arrest him certainly helps." I smiled, but he didn't match my smile. Maybe because I'd sort of kind of ignored his advice when he was representing my grandpa and had ended up getting my grandpa arrested because of it. Or maybe that's just how he was.

A Crazy Cat Lady and Canine Crunchies

Jamie came out from the kitchen to join us, rebraiding her long brown hair as she did so. She had a smudge of flour on her cheek and another one on the tip of her nose making her look impossibly adorable. "Mr. Maxwell? Jamie Green. Nice to meet you."

He actually smiled at her.

(I figured that was a good thing. It helps when your attorney actually likes you, but I still felt a little bitter that he hadn't smiled at me when I said hi.)

He glanced around, pausing pointedly on Greta. "It would be best if we could have this conversation in private."

"I can leave." Greta closed her laptop. "But first I would like to meet this man." She came over to us, hand extended. "Greta VanVeldenstein."

"Mason Maxwell. I believe I've dealt with your nephew and your husband a few times on the land development deal they're planning."

"Ah, yes. Wilhelm has dreams. But not much else, sadly to say. My husband hopes to save him from certain failure."

I stared at her. Even if that was true, who says that to a stranger?

Mason Maxwell took it in stride. "Well, hopefully between your husband and myself we can make that happen."

She nodded, but it was clear she didn't believe it. "You should come for dinner. My husband would like that." She glanced at Jamie and me before adding, "You and your wife?"

"No wife. Just me."

She smiled. "This is sad. But you would like a wife someday?"

If she hadn't kept looking at us I would have almost enjoyed seeing how uncomfortable her questions made him. Who knew that someone could ruffle Mason Maxwell?

"I...Yes. Someday. I just haven't met the right woman yet."

That was a good excuse. I'd have to use that one myself. (Except it was a lie, of course.)

"Good. Then I will find you a wife." As Greta patted his arm he flinched,

A Crazy Cat Lady and Canine Crunchies

but I wasn't sure if it was because of her intent to find him a wife or her touching him so casually.

I stepped forward and gently steered her away. "Well then, Greta. Now that you have your latest matchmaking assignment, we better get started with our meeting. See you tomorrow?"

She nodded. "Yes. I will see you tomorrow."

CHAPTER 10

I walked her to the door and locked it while Jamie locked the other side. We joined Mason Maxwell at a table in the center of the barkery where there was lots of room.

"Would you like something to eat?" Jamie asked. "I make a really good cinnamon roll. Or we have soup and panini I could heat up for you."

"Actually, lunch would be great. I was caught in meetings earlier and only managed to eat a granola bar for lunch. I have heard good things about this place. Time I tried it out myself."

Jamie beamed at him and hurried to the kitchen to make him up a plate of food.

I stared at him awkwardly, not quite sure what to do. He wasn't exactly the type for small talk. "Um, why don't I get you a copy of the emotional support animal certificate Janice Fletcher provided us. You can look that over while Jamie heats up your lunch."

"Yes. Excellent."

"Okay then."

I ran to the back, grabbed the document, gave it to him, and then hurried back to the kitchen to keep Jamie company. I simply didn't know what to do with a man like Mason Maxwell. He was so...formal. It wasn't his money that put me off, it was the stick up his butt.

(Sorry. I know. That's rude. But someone who always has perfect posture and never has a thing out of place just...It's not natural. It's not human.)

While I waited I heated myself up a cinnamon roll and grabbed a Coke from the mini fridge. What can I say? My version of the four food groups is a little different than the average person's.

I watched Mason Maxwell from the edge of the doorway where I didn't think he could see.

"What are you doing?" Jamie came to stand next to me and peeked over my shoulder.

"He scares me. He's very intense. Do you know when he met Fancy she wouldn't even go near him? He told me that dogs were pack animals and that you just had to show them who was the alpha."

She laughed. "I would've liked to see that. And he's not that bad is he? He seems very smart. And kind."

I frowned at her. "He's definitely smart. Scary smart. And that's definitely what you want in a lawyer. But..." I shivered. "Kind? Where'd you get that from?"

"I don't know. Something in his eyes maybe."

I snorted.

Jamie turned away to remove Mason's sandwich from the sandwich press and put it on a plate, adding a small bowl of tomato soup to go along with it. I grabbed my cinnamon roll and followed her to the table.

A Crazy Cat Lady and Canine Crunchies

Mason Maxwell eyed my food choices with a raised eyebrow, but didn't say anything. Good thing. He might intimidate me, but I would defend my sugary food choices to the grave. (Yeah, yeah, make the funny comment about how someone who eats like me probably **will** die from those choices. I'll wait.)

Jamie ran back to the kitchen for a fresh cup of coffee while Mason took his first bites of food. When she returned he gave her a hundred-watt smile that so surprised me I almost fell out of my chair. "This is delicious. I may have to start coming here every day."

(Unlikely. He lived at least twenty minutes away and worked from home as far as I knew.)

"You'd be welcome, of course." Jamie flashed her dimples at him.

I stared at them, wondering what exactly was going on. Did they **like** each other? And if so, what did I think about that? I mean, Mason Maxwell was certainly better than Lucas Dean, but...he was Mason Maxwell. My light-hearted but fierce friend deserved better than this intense man with his too-perfect shoes. I mean, really, who wears a pair of Italian loafers in a Colorado mountain town. This wasn't Vail or Aspen. This was Bakerstown. Buy a good pair of hiking boots, would ya?

"Before we get too far with using your legal help," I said, "I think I should warn you we're kind of limited in terms of funds. So taking her to court or something like that is probably not an option."

He took another bite of his food and chewed it thoroughly before responding, his enjoyment of the food evident. "We can work something out. Janice Fletcher has created difficulties for me in the past. It would be nice to be able to repay that." He nodded towards his food. "Actually, as long as you are willing to provide me with lunch on a regular basis, I would say that should cover the costs."

I stared at him. I'd seen the bill he sent my grandpa and it was not cheap. We'd be feeding him for years. But that would be a lot easier to cover than a big whopping bill.

"Are you sure?"

"Yes. Consider it pro bono work with a twist."

Jamie flashed him another smile. "You have a deal."

"Good."

🐾 🐾 🐾

It turned out that Janice Fletcher's emotional support cat was not in fact allowed into the café and barkery. Only a legitimate service animal had to be accommodated in a restaurant in Colorado, and only dogs and miniature horses qualified. So no cats.

Maybe Janice could take her little bevy of protestors to the state capitol and leave me alone for a while.

I was so happy I could've kissed Mason Maxwell. (Well, maybe not that happy. I still found him very off-putting. Jamie could've though. She was all googly eyed over him.)

"So that settles it then." I sat back, wondering why he'd driven all this way out here just to tell us that.

"Not exactly."

"What do you mean?"

Mason Maxwell leveled a gaze at me that had me feeling decidedly foolish. "There is the court of law and then there is the court of public opinion. You already saw the damage Ms. Fletcher did with that newspaper article about how you wanted to keep locals out of your store."

"But that turned out fine because Jamie just gave them all free cinnamon rolls, so now we have more customers than ever."

"You lucked out last time. But will you the next time Janice Fletcher gets her nephew to write a smear article about this place? The woman is relentless. Other women knit, Janice Fletcher makes it her mission to destroy people."

That didn't sound good.

Jamie drummed her fingers on the table. "So she won't back down even though the law is on our side."

"No. I do not believe she will. Once she realizes this attempt failed, she will try to come at you some other way."

A Crazy Cat Lady and Canine Crunchies

"What other way?" I asked. She'd already protested and served us with this fake letter. What was left?

He shook his head. "I don't know. All I know is that Janice Fletcher does not quit. So if there is anything, anything at all that you have been letting slide, now is the time to fix it. You do not want to have any sort of weakness she can exploit."

"What is her deal?" I demanded. "Seriously. It sounds like the world would be a much better place if she'd just drop dead."

Mason Maxwell leveled his gray-eyed stare at me. "Ms. Carver I would suggest that you keep any wishes for someone to drop dead to yourself. Our conversations are protected by attorney-client privilege, but it is simply a good habit to adopt to never publicly wish for the death of another person."

I snorted. "Like I'm going to kill her. Honestly. Plus, she looks perfectly healthy to me. That old bat will be torturing people for decades."

"You saw with your grandfather that perception matters more than reality.

Do not make the same mistake he did."

"Fine. I hope she lives a long and healthy life of making everyone around her miserable. And I hope we're still in the midst of cat and dog wars a decade from now. Happy?"

"Maggie." Jamie frowned at me. "He's just trying to help."

I pressed my lips together and nodded. I knew that, but a part of me was very much done with his condescending attitude. "Okay then. We'll make sure everything is buttoned up and perfect. Thank you for coming out here and giving us such useful advice."

I stood up.

Neither Mason Maxwell nor Jamie joined me.

With a small huff I gathered up the empty plates and took them to the kitchen. Let them do whatever they were doing. I needed to look for any signs of weakness that Janice Fletcher could exploit.

CHAPTER 11

The whole way home I tried to figure out exactly what Janice Fletcher's next move was going to be. And just how much of a spark there'd been between Jamie and Mason Maxwell. And how much that did or did not upset me. Of course I wanted my best friend to be happy, but Mason Maxwell?

Only as I opened the front door did I remember that my grandpa had invited Matt over for dinner. There he was, seated on the brown couch in the living room, Fancy curled up at his side. He looked more at home there than I ever did. And worse yet, Fancy didn't even bother to get down to come see me when I walked in. She barely lifted her head off her paws.

Aleksa Baxter

You know it's a bad day when even your dog is mad at you.

"Hey, Maggie." Matt toasted me with the beer in his hand.

"Hey. Forgot you were coming over tonight. Sorry I'm so late." My grandpa came out of the kitchen with a big casserole dish in his hands and I gave him a quick kiss on the cheek. "I really am. But this couldn't wait."

He'd set the dining room table with my grandma's best china, but no wine glasses this time. Seems it was going to be a beer kind of night. (Which was honestly just fine with me. I'll drink a glass of wine, no problem, but when given the choice I usually go for a nice porter or brown ale of some sort instead of wine.)

"Can I help?" I asked.

"You can grab the salad from the kitchen," he grumbled, clearly not happy with me.

I grabbed the salad and a bottle of ranch dressing. If Matt wanted something else he was just going to have to suck it up because ranch was the only dressing choice in our household. We didn't even have vinegar around to make oil and vinegar.

By the time I made it to the table they were both seated and waiting for me. So was Fancy. She'd sat herself down by my chair and proceeded to drool a nice little puddle onto the floor. She's not much of a drooler under normal circumstances, but put food near her and she becomes a faucet.

I set the salad and dressing on the table and turned back towards the kitchen. "Start without me."

"What are you doing, Maggie May? Everything's already on the table."

"I forgot Fancy's sharing plate."

"Got one right here," Matt called.

I turned to see him set a small plate in front of her and drop a piece of turkey from the casserole on it. As my heart did a little flip I wondered why he had to be so good with dogs. Or at least with my dog. It wasn't fair.

My grandpa grunted. He did not like the fact that I fed Fancy from the table. In his world dogs were supposed to only eat dog food. And live outside. Or, at most, come into the laundry area. They were most definitely not supposed to have their own plate at meals. Nor were they supposed to sleep on the couch or have five different dog beds. But if I had to choose between making Fancy happy and making my grandpa happy, well, Fancy was going to win out each and every time. At least on the small things.

Matt, ever the diplomat, asked, "So, why were you late tonight? You said it couldn't be helped?"

"Two words. Janice Fletcher. Do you know that woman showed up at the barkery today claiming that her cat Pookums is an emotional support animal?"

Matt and my grandpa both laughed.

"It's not funny. I cannot have cats in that store."

"Why not?" Matt asked. "It's just one cat. And, no offense, but you're pretty slow most of the time. I figure you'd welcome the extra customer."

I glared at him. All I wanted was for one frickin' person to agree with me.

A Crazy Cat Lady and Canine Crunchies

"Just one cat, huh? Did you know she wants to let her cat roam free? That's not even sanitary. And if a dog goes after her cat that could be dangerous. I'd probably get sued. Not to mention I am very, very allergic to cats. It's a dog barkery, for crying out loud, not a cat café."

My grandpa studied me across the table. "So Janice Fletcher has her sights on you, does she?"

"Seems so. And Mason Maxwell said she's not the type to give up until she's ruined us."

"True. She's taken more than one business in this county down. It doesn't help that that nephew of hers is willing to print any slanderous story she asks him to."

He spent the next ten minutes telling us horror stories about Janice Fletcher. Seems she'd even caused one poor store owner to be beaten by a customer who believed her nephew when he printed a story insinuating the man was a sex trafficker.

A sex trafficker? In Baker Valley, Colorado? Population not big enough

for that sort of thing? I don't think
so.

"It sounds to me like the world
would be a better place if she'd just
drop dead and die." I stabbed at a
piece of carrot on my plate and sent
it shooting across the table. My
grandpa caught it and threw it under
the table to Fancy.

"That's a little redundant, isn't it?"
Matt teased. "I'd figure it would be
enough for her to just drop dead."

I shoved a forkful of food into my
mouth and glared him down as I
chewed on it.

"Ouch. You're in a serious mood
tonight."

"I just can't get a break. I mean, I
moved up here to take care of him." I
nodded towards my grandpa. "And he
doesn't want my help."

"That's right." My grandpa nodded.

"I opened a store with my best
friend but now she's all caught up in
finding someone and getting married.
And then every time I think I'm going
to make some progress in turning the
barkery into a real business
something like this happens."

A Crazy Cat Lady and Canine Crunchies

"Jamie's looking to settle down, huh?" Matt looked thoughtful as he took his next bite of food.

"Don't tell her I told you that!"

"She have anyone in mind?"

Was he seriously interested in her? I mean, I wouldn't blame him if he was, but...Ah! Life. It was not being very kind to me.

"I don't know. She doesn't want to talk to me about it."

I glared at the table, not able to look at him as I added, "If you want to throw your hat in the ring, you'd probably have a pretty good shot. You'd certainly be a better match for her than Lucas Dean or Mason Maxwell."

"Mason Maxwell?" My grandpa snorted. "Well, he does have money, I'll give him that."

Fortunately, the conversation turned to just how much of the valley Mason's family controlled compared to how much of the valley Janice Fletcher's family controlled. It seems they were always warring back and forth, one or the other trying to get the upper hand. Had been for close to two hundred years.

After we'd finished up our meal Matt helped me take the dishes into the kitchen while my grandpa went to fetch the Scrabble board. He's obsessed with that game. And last time we'd played Matt had won, which my grandpa could not let stand unchallenged.

I scooped the remaining casserole into a plastic container and handed it to Matt. "Here. Better than whatever awful food you're fixing yourself, I'm sure."

"Hey, now. Canned tuna and potato chips is a perfectly good meal."

I shuddered. "Please tell me you've at least discovered the wonders of microwave meals? A lot of them actually have vegetables in them, you know."

He shrugged one shoulder. "Vegetables are over-rated."

"You do realize that you don't have to live the life of the lonely pathetic bachelor, right? I'd bet that woman the other day isn't the only one trying to fix you up with a daughter or a niece or a granddaughter. Play your cards right you could get a lot of good meals out of it."

"Yeah, but they'd all come with expectations. And awkward conversations." He set the container on the counter. "Only reason I come over here for dinner is because you were so clear about how, what was it? There are more important things in life than being some man's wife?"

I almost softened that statement, but stopped myself in time. "You know, that German woman at the barkery, Greta? She's like Little Miss Matchmaker. I'd be careful you don't let her know you're single or she'll be trying to set you up, too."

"She's going to find you someone?" He leaned against the counter, crossing his arms.

"So she says. Of course, her idea of setting me up is finding me a nice, old man with lots of money who will die soon. She thinks that's the kind of man who makes an ideal **first** husband. I can marry for love later."

He laughed. It was a deep, rich sound that made my toes tingle.

I bit my lip. "So why is it you don't take anyone up on all those other invitations? Not looking to settle down?"

"I can't exactly make plans with a woman when I'm not sure where I want to be a year from now."

"So not planning on sticking around?" My stomach dropped a little at the thought of him moving away.

He rubbed at his chin. "I don't know. I mean, it made sense to come back here after I got out of the service and my dad died. There was a lot to take care of and the valley was really the only place I'd ever called home. Bob offered me the position as a cop and it all just fell into place. Maybe too easily, you know?"

"So if you don't stay here, what would you do?"

"I might re-enlist. They've offered me a pretty good bonus."

It was all I could do not to step forward and grab his arms and tell him not to go, but my grandpa saved me from making a fool of myself when he called for us from the living room.

A Crazy Cat Lady and Canine Crunchies

As Matt went to join him I hung back, trying to control the emotions coursing through me. I knew if I tried to date him it would be a disaster, but I didn't want to lose him either. It wasn't often I felt that little spark with someone. I shook myself. Hard.

I had priorities. And falling in love was not one of them.

"Anyone want ice cream?" I shouted.

"Yeah, give me a bowl," my grandpa shouted back. "Matt? You want some? Maggie May, make it two."

"Alright. Will do."

By the time I'd scooped out three bowls of ice cream and taken them into the dining room, I was back under control. That didn't mean I wasn't thinking about Matt leaving to re-enlist for the rest of the night.

I was.

CHAPTER 12

The next morning I was NOT in a good mood. I wanted Janice Fletcher to die a horrible fiery death and I wanted Officer Matthew Barnes to stay in Baker Valley and smile at me with that great smile of his and come over for dinner with my grandpa and yet not actually ask me to make an emotional commitment I wasn't capable of making.

To make myself feel better I'd decided it was about time Fancy was allowed to come back to work with me, but she was so wound up by the chance to get out of the house and maybe see Lulu—Jamie's golden retriever puppy—that she wouldn't sit down the whole drive to the barkery and kept crying right in my ear.

A Crazy Cat Lady and Canine Crunchies

So when I picked up a copy of the **Baker Valley Gazette** early that morning and saw the headline, **How Clean Is Your Favorite Restaurant?** I was ready to hurt someone. Especially because it was accompanied by a photo of a bakery box with our logo on it sitting on the top of a grimy pile of trash. The article itself toed the line—there was no actual mention of our store—but that photo sure implied a lot of things it shouldn't.

After the third customer walked in and glanced around the place as if looking for a mouse to scurry out from the corner, I'd had it. "Jamie. You're on your own for a bit. I'll be back."

"Wait. Where are you going?"

I waved the paper at her. "To deal with this."

"No! Let Mason Maxwell deal with it. You stay here."

I shook my head. "They had no right."

"And he'll deal with it. There will be a retraction in the paper tomorrow morning and probably one up on the website this afternoon."

"Doesn't matter. The damage is done. We should sue for lost sales."

Jamie shook her head. "We don't need to sue anyone, Maggie."

I started towards the door again. Jamie was my best friend and I loved her to pieces, but sometimes she was just a little too forgiving.

"Maggie. Promise me you won't confront Peter Nielsen. Let Mason handle this."

"Promise." That was easy enough to do. Peter Nielsen wasn't my target. I was going to the source: Janice Fletcher.

I shoved the door open, the bells at the top making a discordant jangle and stormed to my van, muttering to myself about how the world really would be a better place if some people would just up and die already.

I'd never been to Janice Fletcher's house, but that's the interesting thing about living in a small town. (Or in this case a series of small towns.) You pretty much know where all the major players live. And Janice

A Crazy Cat Lady and Canine Crunchies

Fletcher's house was hard to miss. It was a tactless monstrosity that dominated the hillside just outside of Bakerstown. She'd cut down all the trees on her lot so that it looked like some sort of blight had hit the area. The house itself was hideous. It was a giant pimple on the face of the world.

Just like its owner.

I banged on her door, not caring that it wasn't even seven in the morning yet. If she could show up to protest my store that early, she could answer her damned door.

She finally answered on the fifth knock. She had her hair up in rollers and a tatty red robe on. Her house slippers were bulky things with little cat's heads on the end. And she had Pookums in her arms. Well, that's what I thought at least. Until I stepped into her house and realized that there were at least five other cats in that house. They meowed at us in some sort of crazy cat cacophony.

"What's up with your cats?"

"It's breakfast time. You interrupted my feeding them."

They wound their way around her legs and mine, crying out for their food. I sneezed. "Well go ahead and feed them then."

"No. You'll be gone soon enough."

I glanced around the place. There was a double-spiral staircase leading to an upstairs balcony. The main entranceway stretched towards an extremely large living room. At the far end of the entryway was an open doorway with what looked to be stairs leading downward. A large dining room was off to my right with a kitchen barely visible at the end.

The house would've been nice inside if it hadn't been forced to suffer from Janice Fletcher's bad taste. Honestly, some colors just do not go together.

The cats continued to cry, growing louder and louder as they wrapped themselves around her feet and mine. I heard a crashing sound from the direction of the kitchen. Yet another cat? How many did one person need?

A Crazy Cat Lady and Canine Crunchies

(I know. Cats are wonderful and lovely and why wouldn't you have ten million of them if you could. Yeah, yeah.)

I was already regretting the anger that had brought me to her door, but it was too late to back down. "That article this morning was you, wasn't it?"

"Of course it was. And the health inspection will be, too." She gave me such a nasty smile I wanted to punch her teeth out.

(I swear I'm not normally violent like that, but that woman just pushed all of my buttons.)

"Jamie and I keep a clean shop. There's nothing for an inspector to find."

She stroked Pookum's back as she stepped closer to me. "I wouldn't be so sure..."

I sneezed and stepped back. "Did you do something to our store?"

She just smiled at me.

"Did you? What did you do? Why do you have it in for us?" I wanted to grab her and shake her. But I didn't. I swear, I did not lay a single hand on her.

"You should leave now. I have to feed the cats."

"You did something. What?"

"Close the door on your way out." She turned and sauntered towards the kitchen.

I'll admit, there was a small part of me that wanted to run after her and beat her sanctimonious brains in. But I didn't.

I swear.

Instead, I raced out the door and ran to my van. I needed to get back to the barkery as soon as possible. I needed to figure out what Janice Fletcher had done to our store before the health inspector arrived, because you just knew after that article that we'd be getting a surprise inspection.

I was driving so fast as I left I almost side-swiped a green sedan that had just turned onto her block. Right after that I had to slam on my brakes as a man jogged in front of my car wearing a hoodie with the hood up and long sweat pants. I wasn't a big fan of being observed

A Crazy Cat Lady and Canine Crunchies

when I exercised either, but that man was taking it to an extreme.

CHAPTER 13

I was almost back to the store when I realized I'd handled that all wrong.

(That's my curse. I act in the moment and then think it through later and second-guess everything. There's always a better way things could've gone. Too bad I can never think of the right thing to say or do in the actual moment.)

I whipped a U-turn and headed back to Janice's house, but got stuck behind some touristy RV that was going at least five under the speed limit. As I quietly muttered to myself about what they should really test for on driver's tests and how some people should simply not be allowed to drive, I tried to think of what I was going to say when I got back to Janice's house.

A Crazy Cat Lady and Canine Crunchies

I mean, she clearly had it in for me. How exactly did I expect to convince her to let up? For one horrible moment I wondered if there was someone else I could point her towards. People like that always need someone to go after, so chances are she wasn't going to leave me alone until she'd either destroyed me or found a better target.

But that wasn't nice. No one else deserved to go through what I was.

I sat outside her house for a long, long moment wondering whether it was worth it to even attempt to reason with her. But finally I pulled myself out of the car and walked up her front steps. I had to try. It wasn't just me this was impacting. It was Jamie and our store and Fancy.

For their sakes I had to solve the puzzle of Janice Fletcher.

🐾 🐾 🐾

The front door was slightly ajar when I reached it, but I figured that was my fault. She hadn't walked me out, after all, so I must not have pulled it closed tightly enough.

I pushed the door open and stepped inside. "Janice? Janice, it's Maggie. Can we talk?"

There was a loud crashing sound from the direction of the kitchen. I headed in that direction through the dining room, but all I found was a wet cast iron pan in the sink and a large plate on the counter with cats huddled around it eating. Whoever had put down their food wasn't the most fastidious person in the world, that's for sure. It looked like someone had just opened about five cans of cat food and dumped them in the middle of that plate without any care or concern.

Odd, but who am I to judge how someone else feeds their pets.

"Janice?" I slowly made my way toward the living room, listening for any sign of where she might be. Knowing my luck she was in the bathroom or shower or something equally embarrassing and awkward.

There was a creaking sound from the direction of the doorway to the basement, so I moved in that direction. "Janice? It's Maggie Carver.

A Crazy Cat Lady and Canine Crunchies

Remember me? I was just here. Can we talk?"

I walked through the living room, still seeing no sign of her, but when I turned towards the door to the basement, I saw one of her cat slippers in the doorway. I stepped closer. "Janice?"

One of the cats brushed past me and made its way down the stairs. I heard that creaking sound again. Must be a bad step.

I moved to the top of the stairs and looked down into the darkness, but I couldn't see anything. Not really wanting to, but compelled to do so, I turned the light on.

And saw Janice Fletcher at the bottom of the stairs, a cat sitting on her chest meowing loudly.

I knew I should call 9-1-1. Maybe she was still alive. (Although, no. I won't go into details but it was pretty clear she hadn't survived the fall down those steps.) Still, someone should. The woman was dead after all, and she couldn't just stay down there forever.

But...

And this is horrible. And, yes, it was a mistake. But see, the last time I'd called the cops when I found a dead body my grandpa had ended up almost going to prison for a murder he didn't commit. And now there I was, in Janice Fletcher's house, with a reason to want her dead, and absolutely no alibi because I'd been there both right before and right after she died.

And it was probably just a frickin' accident caused by one of those ridiculous cats of hers or those cat slippers she insisted on wearing. And all that would happen if I called the cops was I'd have to explain what I was doing there and they'd be bound to wonder if it was really an accident with me found practically standing over her dead body.

But I figured if someone like a neighbor or her nephew were to drop by later and just find her they'd easily see the truth of the matter, right?

I know. But that's the way I figured it in the moment. I told you—I have my best thoughts after things happen, not during.

A Crazy Cat Lady and Canine Crunchies

I sneezed and heard a loud crash from the basement. Probably another one of her cats—they were all over the place—but that decided me. I needed to just get the heck out of there. I did not want someone coming along and finding me at the top of Janice Fletcher's stairs with her dead body at the bottom. Plus, if I didn't leave soon I was going to be sneezing and sniffling for the rest of the day.

Not to mention, the whole thing was just creeping me out. Big, dark house. Lots of cats. Dead body. It was a good opening scene to a horror movie if you asked me.

I know. I should've called the cops.

And if you ever find a dead body, definitely do so. But I didn't.

CHAPTER 14

I turned the light back off and carefully let myself out the front door, using the bottom of my t-shirt to grip the handle so I wouldn't leave any prints. And this time I made sure it had actually closed properly. Didn't need all of those cats out wandering the neighborhood. (They looked like indoor cats to me, although don't ask me why I thought that about them.)

As I walked towards the van I looked around to see if there was anyone around who could testify that they'd seen me—not that I knew what I'd do if there was, I wasn't a killer after all—but I saw no one.

I drove back to the store, grateful this time to be stuck behind some slow-moving tourist. Halfway there the shakes set in and I wondered if

I'd made the right decision. It wasn't too late. I could still call it in, but what would I say?

"Yeah, sorry. Found a dead body. Not the person who killed them. Decided to leave rather than tell you about it. Now I'm feeling a little guilty about that choice, so figured I'd better let you know so you can swing by there before her cats eat her face."

I know, the cats had just been fed, but all those horrible stories of single women who'd died alone at home and been eaten by their cats were running through my head. (Okay, so maybe that's only ever happened to one person, but in my mind there were hundreds of them.)

I chewed on my thumbnail as I wondered if anyone would even miss Janice Fletcher. Would they miss her enough to swing by her house? If they did, would they go in? Would they look in the basement?

I parked in front of the barkery, still not sure what to do. I thought about calling Mason Maxwell. He was my lawyer, after all. But there was a foolish part of me that was just hoping it would all go away. Janice Fletcher was dead, which meant no more harassment. Someone would find her eventually, I was sure. And then it would all be over.

Right?

Yeah, no.

CHAPTER 15

"Where did you go?" Jamie asked as soon as I walked through the door.

"I just drove around a bit." I set my purse down in the office, downed a couple of Benadryl, and snagged a cinnamon roll that was on a cooling tray.

(I know, I lied to her and that wasn't very nice, but Jamie has a moral center that would've demanded calling the cops, so it was better to just not involve her. I don't lie often, if that's any consolation.)

I took a moment to savor the spicy sweet taste of the cinnamon roll while I pondered whether I could convince Jamie to start making chocolate croissants like you find in France and, if I could, whether I would be okay with the twenty-plus pounds I'd put on as a result. I was pretty sure that was an okay tradeoff. Life is meant to be lived after all.

"I've been thinking," I said. "I bet that article triggers a health inspection. We should clean this place. Top to bottom. Inside out."

Jamie glanced towards the front where our latest shop assistant was ringing up a customer. "This is the busiest time of the morning."

"Not at the barkery. You guys keep handling the customers, I'll do the cleaning."

"You? Are you okay? You hate to clean."

"I know. But needs must and all."

I really do hate cleaning, as some of my college roommates learned the hard way. I'm not filthy or anything. I have a very sensitive nose so anything that stinks does not last. But it's just not something I take joy in and I have a high dust tolerance. Or so it would seem given the complaints of those who do seem to enjoy cleaning.

A Crazy Cat Lady and Canine Crunchies

Anyway. I printed out a copy of the health inspection form and got to work. And I almost enjoyed it. It was nice to have some mindless physical activity to distract me from the mess of that morning. Not that I wasn't thinking about it, just that I at least had something to do with my hands while I thought.

About half an hour later Mason Maxwell walked in looking like some big town billionaire instead of the small-town lawyer he really was. I bet the man didn't even own a pair of tennies. Or hiking boots.

Jamie beamed at him from behind the counter. "Hey, Mason. What can I get you?"

Mason, huh? Like they were good buddies or something. I wondered what he'd do if I called him Mason. Probably frown at me like I'd broken some unspoken rule of etiquette. Not that I wanted to be on a first-name basis with him anyway.

He smiled at her. It almost made him approachable. "Let me try one of those cinnamon rolls I've heard so much about."

"Absolutely. And a coffee?"

I knew that tone of voice. My friend was most definitely interested. I sighed. When was she going to date a man who'd actually be a good choice for her?

I scrubbed at the table I was working on a little harder than was necessary as I wondered what had brought him by. Had Jamie called him about the article? Or had he come by on his own?

"Mr. Maxwell." I set my bleach bucket under the counter as Jamie went to the back to specially prepare his cinnamon roll.

"Ms. Carver."

"I was meaning to call you today. Did you see that article in the paper about sanitation issues at local restaurants?"

"No, I hadn't had a chance to read the paper yet this morning."

Jamie handed him his cinnamon roll. "Maggie, why don't you let him eat his breakfast before you start in on that?"

"Because the sooner Peter Nielsen issues a retraction, the better."

A Crazy Cat Lady and Canine Crunchies

"It's not like he named us."

"No. He just included a picture of one of our bakery boxes right next to the headline." I slammed a copy of the paper down on the counter for Mason Maxwell to see.

Jamie's competent as competent can be and completely unruffleable, but she's also not one for open conflict. Even when it's warranted like it was this time.

Mason quickly scanned the text, noted the picture, and nodded. "That is definitely worthy of a retraction. I will give him a visit as soon as I finish here." He took a bite of his cinnamon roll and closed his eyes for a moment in pleasure. "You are an excellent cook, Jamie."

"Thank you." Jamie blushed and ducked her head. I'm pretty sure she even batted her eyelashes at him.

I decided it was time for me to get to work in the kitchen. It's not that I objected to her liking Mason Maxwell. (Although I couldn't really see it myself. He's so...stiff.) But I just hate to see the way women contort themselves around a man they like.

All of a sudden it's batted eyes, girly giggles, and ducked heads. I know it's just biology at work, but doesn't mean I have to enjoy watching it.

(And, no, I'm not immune to doing it myself, which kind of makes it worse, really. To hate it and do it anyway and then hate yourself for doing it. Not that I really hate myself ever, but you know what I mean.)

Anyway.

An hour later when I checked back on Jamie, Mason was gone and she was in conversation with some well-dressed man I'd never seen before, both of them leaning on the counter and talking softly. The man was tall, ice-blond, and dressed all in black, right down to his fancy shoes which looked like a black leather version of the ones Mason Maxwell wore.

Ugh. It was contagious. Before I knew it the whole town was going to be overrun by men in pressed slacks, soft sweaters, and fancy shoes. Honestly, what was wrong with blue jeans?

"Maggie, this is Don. Don this is my co-owner Maggie. Don's in town for business for a few days. Said we might see him around since he'll need a place to hang out that isn't a dingy little hotel room."

Like this man was ever going to stay in a dingy little hotel room. He probably had a suite at the resort. Or an Airbnb rental that was five-hundred a night.

"Nice to meet you, Don. Mind if I steal my business partner away for a minute?"

"No. Not at all."

He made his way to a corner table on the café side as I turned to Jamie. "Is Mr. Maxwell going to talk to Peter Nielsen for us?"

"Of course. He said he would."

"Just making sure."

"Why don't you like him? I mean, he's smart. He's funny. He's good-looking."

Mason Maxwell, funny? And good-looking? I mean, sure, if you like Sean Connery in his older incarnation and it isn't about the accent. But...

"He's a little old, don't you think?"

"He's not even fifty. And aren't you the one always telling me I need to improve my taste in men?"

"Well, yeah." I glanced towards Don who was trying to listen in without listening in. "But someone like that guy over there was more what I had in mind."

She winked at me. "No rule that says I can't date them both. It's just a little crush, after all. No point pinning my hopes on just one guy who may or may not be interested. Speaking of..." She left me to go join Don at his table.

As I watched them laugh and lean close, I wondered what it's like to be that person. The one that can see the whole dating world as a smorgasbord to be sampled from. Someone who doesn't mind when they find that yet another person is not to their liking after all. Or is but isn't interested. Someone who just lets it all roll past them and enjoys it for what it is.

Me, I take all of it far too seriously. Partially because they don't always shake off when I find they're not what I wanted and then it's just awkward and uncomfortable when

A Crazy Cat Lady and Canine Crunchies

they keep calling and won't go away. Or worse, just showing up. Only way to avoid that is to date complete strangers which has its own set of risks. (Seriously, I watch way too many true crime shows. And police procedurals. I'm sure the majority of men are not stalkers or crazy rapists, but watch enough of those shows and you start to wonder.)

But enough about my dysfunctions.

By the time the health inspector showed up for his "surprise" inspection a couple hours later—right in the middle of our lunch rush, I might add—we were ready and waiting and passed with flying colors.

It's good to be prepared.

Unfortunately, when the cops showed up two hours after that? I was anything but prepared to see them.

CHAPTER 16

Matt walked through the door first, Officer Clark right behind him. I knew it wasn't a social visit by the way Officer Clark's hand rested on his gun as he glared at me. What did he think I was going to do? Pull a shotgun from under the counter and shout, "You're never going to take me alive?"

Please.

"Ms. Carver." Matt stopped about five feet away. Ouch, that hurt.

"Officer Barnes. Officer Clark. How can I help you?"

"Were you aware that Janice Fletcher is dead?"

Tricky question, that. If I answered yes, then I was admitting I'd been in her house and seen her dead body and done nothing about it. If I answered no and someone had seen me then I would have started off what was clearly a police investigation on a very, very bad foot.

I knew what Mason Maxwell would say: "Shut your mouth and call your lawyer." But since when did I listen to good common sense?

Jamie came over. "What's wrong? What's going on?"

Matt stepped closer. "Ms. Carver. Were you aware that Janice Fletcher is dead?"

Officer Clark sighed in disgust. "You know she is. The neighbor saw her running out of there."

I met Matt's blue eyes. "I didn't kill her."

"But you knew she was dead?"

I shrugged slightly before turning to Jamie. "I need you to call Mason Maxwell for me." I turned back to Matt. "Am I under arrest? Or do you just need to question me?"

"Maggie..."

Officer Clark stepped forward. "We should put her under arrest."

I ignored him and kept my attention focused on Matt. "I'll meet you at the station in half an hour if I'm not under arrest. I didn't kill her. I'm not sure anyone did. But I'm not going to say more without my lawyer present."

Matt nodded. "We'll meet you at the station."

Officer Clark sent me one last snarly look but at least they both left without handcuffing me and dragging me after them.

Jamie stepped closer. "Maggie, what was that about?"

"You heard him. Janice Fletcher is dead. And they obviously suspect me."

She grabbed my arm as I tried to step past her. "Did you do it?"

"Do you really think I'm capable of that?"

"I think anyone's capable of anything if the circumstances are right. But if you did do it, I don't think you set out to do it."

"Oh that's a comfort." I pushed past her. "For the record, I would never think you could kill someone."

A Crazy Cat Lady and Canine Crunchies

I grabbed my purse and leashed up Fancy. "Call Mason Maxwell. Tell him to meet me at the jail. I'll swing by my house and tell my grandpa what's happening when I drop Fancy off."

🐾 🐾 🐾

My grandpa was none too pleased when I told him what had brought me home so early, but I told him not to worry it would all be cleared up soon enough. I figured Janice Fletcher had just tripped on one of her eight million cats. Only question was, could anyone prove it?

I figured there had to be some difference in the injuries someone would suffer if they'd tripped down a flight of stairs instead of been shoved down them. It always seems to work the opposite way on those crime shows where they eventually determine that the husband's story of his wife's unfortunate fall down the stairs with her laundry basket was just made up crap.

I certainly hoped so. Because if not clearly someone had seen me running from her house. And not like I had an alibi. I'd been there right before she died **and** right after she died, which meant I might as well have been standing over her body the whole time.

I sat on the floor and buried my face in Fancy's fur, but she quickly pulled away. She loves me, but not enough to let me snuggle all over her. (What can I say, we're a lot alike.)

"I have to go." I pushed myself to my feet. "With any luck I'll be home for dinner. If I'm not, you know where to find me."

My grandpa reached for the non-existent pack of cigarettes in his shirt pocket and then cussed when he remembered he no longer smoked. I grabbed his hand. It was trembling slightly. "Promise me two things. Well, three."

"What?"

"First, you won't smoke because of this." I didn't want to be the cause for him taking it up again, and I still remembered how he'd gone for the pack of cigarettes he kept stashed in his workroom when they came to arrest him.

"Fine. What else?"

A Crazy Cat Lady and Canine Crunchies

"If they do put me in jail, you'll take care of Fancy for me. I'm sure Matt'll help if you need it, but please, take care of her. She's my world."

He nodded. "And three?"

"You'll take care of yourself."

He snorted. "I've been taking care of myself for eighty-two years. I think I can do so for a little while longer."

I gave him a quick, fierce hug. "I hope so."

He grabbed my chin and looked me in the eye. "You better be home for dinner, young lady."

"I'll try." I gave him another hug and rushed out the door before I could start crying.

I'd never messed up that bad in my life and I wasn't sure how I was going to fix it. But I had to somehow, because my grandpa and Fancy needed me, whether either one realized it or not.

CHAPTER 17

Mason Maxwell was waiting for me outside the police station. The station is so close to my grandpa's house I'd decided to walk, so I had a good long time to watch him as I slowly came closer. He was not amused.

"Mr. Maxwell. Jamie reached you I see?"

He nodded. "What is this about?"

"She didn't tell you?"

"I want to hear it from you."

I glanced towards the single-story sandstone building. I could see the receptionist sitting behind her desk, Matt and Officer Clark behind her, watching us through the glass doors.

"Janice Fletcher is dead. I didn't kill her. I honestly think she tripped on one of her cats. But I was in her house this morning around the time of her death."

"Before or after?"

I bit my lip. "Both. But not during."

He stepped closer, his eyes flashing. "What?"

"I went to yell at her about the article in the paper. And then I left. But when I was almost back to the store I decided to go back to her house and see if I could reason with her. She was alive when I left the first time and dead when I returned. Her body was at the bottom of the basement stairs."

"Did you touch the body?"

I shook my head.

"Did you call the cops?"

I shook my head again. "They said a neighbor saw me leaving. I assume that was the first time, when she was still alive."

Mason Maxwell visibly worked to control his anger. It was fascinating to watch, because he was clearly a man of intense passions who managed to rein them in rather than spew them all over the world like I always seem to.

When he was fully under control he held the outer door open for me, ever the gentleman even when he clearly thought his client was a fool. "Best get this over with."

I turned to him before opening the inner door. "Do you want me to answer their questions? Or refuse to speak? What would you like me to do?"

He took a deep, deep breath. "I would like you to not confront people you have publicly stated you wish were dead, but we're past that aren't we?"

"Yes, we are. So what do I do now?"

He pinched the bridge of his nose, clearly thinking through the alternatives. "Officer Barnes likes you?"

"We're friends."

"And they said someone saw you at her house?"

I nodded.

A Crazy Cat Lady and Canine Crunchies

"Then I want you to tell them everything. Be as open and honest as you can be. That may save you from jail, but don't count on it."

With that cheery thought, I opened the inner door and stepped through to begin my very first (but not last, sadly) police interrogation.

🐾 🐾 🐾

Matt and Officer Clark led me past the main portion of the police station where four desks were located, two on each side facing each other, and past two offices with windows that looked out on them.

We went down a short hallway and into a small room. I'd been there before when my grandpa was arrested. It's where Matt, my grandpa, and I had eaten dinner. Somehow I hadn't noticed how cold it was that first visit.

Nor had I noticed the pervasive smell of body odor and stale cigarettes that was only faintly masked by some astringent cleaner.

Nor had I noticed how stiff and uncomfortable the plastic chairs were.

You'd think that making someone as relaxed and comfortable as you could get them would make them more forthcoming, but it seems not. Because I don't think I've ever seen an interrogation room that looks welcoming.

Me, if it were my choice, I'd set up a room like a plush therapist's office with a big mirror on the wall facing the suspect and put two comfortable couches across from each other. I'd make the suspect feel like I was there to help them through this ordeal they found themselves in. **Just let it go. Just tell me what you did and you'll feel so much better.**

Guess that's why I'm not a cop. Or a psychiatrist. Or a priest for that matter.

Matt pulled up the chair directly across from me while Officer Clark paced behind him even though there was another seat for him to sit in.

Mason Maxwell wiped his seat off with a real, live handkerchief before he took a seat next to me. He looked like a fish out of water in his fancy clothes and his country-club manners. I wondered if he'd considered refusing to help me, but it didn't matter at that point. He was there and I was his client and he was going to do what he could.

Matt pressed the button to record the conversation and then introduced himself, Officer Clark, Mason Maxwell, and me. He even advised me of my rights. I could see it was killing him to be there. To think that I'd killed this woman. But he was a man of duty. He'd go where the clues led him, even if they led him to me.

"Ms. Carver. You're aware of your rights. Are you willing to proceed with this interview at this time?" He glanced towards Mason Maxwell.

"We can proceed. I have nothing to hide." I met his stare and held it, willing him to believe in my innocence.

Mason Maxwell placed his hand on the table between us. "My client would like to give a full accounting of her actions this morning. I'd ask that you let her do so before you ask any questions." Smart. Otherwise things would probably deteriorate long before I could get it all out.

Aleksa Baxter

Officer Clark paced the room like a restless panther, but Matt simply nodded. Clearly no need to ask who was good cop, bad cop here. "Whenever you're ready."

I took a deep breath and closed my eyes for a moment, trying to marshal my thoughts. I was going to tell them the truth and all of it, but I didn't need to make myself look like an incredibly horrible person while I was doing so.

I laced my fingers together and set my hands on the table before I started. "Over the past couple of weeks Janice Fletcher has been targeting my business. She has a cat, Pookums, and she wanted to bring it with her into my barkery, which is a bakery for dogs. I told her she couldn't. It wasn't safe for her cat nor was it sanitary to have her cat running loose in our store. She then led a protest of my business and threatened me and my customers until we had to call the cops."

So far all I was doing was giving the cops about ten different motives for killing her. Not like they didn't know it already, though.

128

A Crazy Cat Lady and Canine Crunchies

"After her protest failed she obtained a certificate that declared her cat an emotional support animal. She used that to try to force me to allow her and her cat into my store, but my lawyer reviewed the certificate and the law and informed me that it didn't give her the right to be there."

My throat felt dry and I licked my lips wishing someone would offer me a Coke. I'd have even settled for water at that point, but none was forthcoming, so I coughed a little and continued on as best I could.

"Her nephew runs the local paper, and this morning there was an article in there about restaurants with poor sanitation. It included a picture of a bakery box with our logo next to the headline. The article didn't name us specifically, but it was clear we were the target. And it was clear to me who was behind that article."

I paused to gather my thoughts. Matt hadn't taken his eyes off my face the whole time I was speaking. Officer Clark had stopped his pacing and was standing off to the side, arms crossed, glaring me down like I was worse than the scum on the bottom of his shoe. I quickly turned my attention back to Matt.

"I was very upset by the article. I had been told that Janice Fletcher is capable of destroying people when she decides to do so and I believed that article was another attempt by her to attack my business. So I went over to her place to confront her. I'm not sure exactly what time it was, but I remember thinking to myself that if she could protest my store before seven a.m. then she could darn well answer her door at that time, too."

Mason Maxwell coughed slightly and I glanced at him. He pinched his fingers together in what I assumed was his sign for stick to the facts. But I needed Matt to believe me. Which means I needed him to understand what I'd done and why I'd been there.

I told them about that initial confrontation with Janice and about her cat slippers and how hard those things can be to walk in. (I'd know. My mother, bless her, had bought me more than one pair like them over the years.) I also made sure to point out to them how the cats were meowing and hungry and wrapping themselves around her legs and mine. And how that door to the downstairs had been open when I arrived.

Officer Clark interrupted even though he wasn't supposed to. "Let me see your pants."

I lifted my leg above the edge of the table and sneezed. I'm not normally **that** allergic to cats, but Pookums was a Persian and that particular breed just does me in.

"Ha." He said. "Proof you were there."

I stared at him a long, long moment but refrained from pointing out how my confession that I was there was probably even better evidence in that respect.

"So anyway..." I continued.

I told them how I'd left to get back to the barkery and warn Jamie about the pending health inspection but how I'd changed my mind and turned back around to try once more to reason with Ms. Fletcher. And how I'd found the front door slightly ajar when I returned, so had entered the house looking for her.

"I saw one of her slippers at the top of the stairs to the basement and when I turned on the light for the stairs, I saw her at the bottom. One of her cats was down there with her and she was clearly not moving. I...I thought about calling the cops," I glanced at Officer Clark, "but the last time I found a body and did that my grandpa ended up in jail for a murder he didn't commit. Plus, I thought the whole thing was a terrible accident. That she'd tripped on one of her cats and fallen down the stairs and that someone would find her soon enough. So I left."

Officer Clark slammed his hand on the table. "You want us to believe you didn't push her? I bet you did. I bet you pushed her down those stairs and then left her there to die."

"I didn't push her. And I didn't leave her there to die. She was already dead. You saw the body."

"Liar." He leaned forward until I could smell the bologna he'd had for lunch. "You shoved her down those stairs and then you ran from the house, hoping no one would see you."

"I did not kill Janice Fletcher. She was alive the first time I saw her. And dead when I went back."

"I don't believe you."

"Believe me or not, it's the truth." I leaned back and crossed my arms. They were either going to believe me or they weren't, but I'd told them the truth.

Mason Maxwell leaned forward. "You've heard my client's story. She didn't kill Janice Fletcher. Now, is she under arrest? Or not."

"Not."

Officer Clark glared at Matt for a moment and I thought he was going to override him. He was the more senior officer, after all. But instead he jerked open the door. "Sue needs a sample from those pants. Stay here."

I looked to Matt, but he wasn't quite looking at me. "I swear I didn't kill her."

He nodded, but he still wouldn't look at me. He glanced at his notes.

"The first time you were there it was sometime before seven?"

"Yes."

"And while you were gone she had time to feed her cats."

"Yes. That's what it looked like to me."

"And to fall down the stairs."

I nodded. He pointed to the recorder, so I added. "Yes. Again, that's what it looked like to me."

"And you didn't check to make sure she was dead?"

What do you say to that? It sounds horrible. To have someone who must've only been dead a few minutes at the base of the stairs and not even check that they're breathing, but...

"You saw the body. Would you have thought there was any possible way she was alive?"

He set his pencil down. "Why didn't you call the cops?"

I knew what he was really asking. Why hadn't I called him? Why hadn't I trusted him enough to let him know I was standing in Janice Fletcher's house with her dead body at the bottom of the stairs and that I hadn't done it?

I looked down. I couldn't stand the betrayal I saw in his eyes. "It was a mistake. I see that now. I just...I knew I hadn't killed her. But I knew it looked bad for me to be there so close to when she'd died. And I figured she'd just fallen down the stairs, so not like there was some killer on the loose. It just...It made more sense at the time for me to let someone else find her."

I drummed my fingers on the table, thinking how to say what I wanted to say next. "If no one had found her body within the next day, I would've called and told you. But I figured a woman like that in a house like that and with that many cats probably had a cleaning lady who came through daily. And that if that wasn't the case then Peter Nielsen would probably be calling or dropping by at some point in the day to gloat about his article. Or the health inspector would be. I didn't expect she'd be there long."

He turned off the recording and stood. He still wouldn't quite look at me. "Wait here until Sue comes back. We'll want to take some samples from your pants."

"I already told you I was there."

He finally did look at me, his gaze nailing me to the seat. I wished he hadn't. "People tend to change their stories once they're charged with murder. So we like to get all the evidence we can."

"Fine. Take all the evidence you want. But my story isn't going to change. I was there, but I didn't kill her."

I could see Mason Maxwell shaking his head out of the corner of my eye, but I ignored him. All I wanted in that moment was for Matt to believe me.

"We'll see what the autopsy says." He left, slamming the door behind him.

I glanced at Mason Maxwell. "Well, good news. I'm not under arrest."

"Yet." He stood. "Don't say anything to anyone without me present. I need to make some calls."

A Crazy Cat Lady and Canine Crunchies

After he'd left I stared at the far wall wishing I'd brought a book with me to pass the time. I wondered if they would've let me read it. Or if making me sit in that nasty-smelling room in that uncomfortable chair without water for almost an hour was part of their interrogation strategy. Like I'd really break down and confess my sins over an hour of discomfort.

Since I had nothing else to do I spent the time thinking through every single detail of that morning. Had I left the front door slightly ajar when I raced out of there? And if I had, why hadn't Janice closed it? And had that sound I'd heard from the kitchen when I returned been one of the cats? I'd assumed it was, but what if it wasn't. And the sound from the basement?

Could someone else have been there?

No...

At the end I came to the same conclusion as before: Janice Fletcher had tripped on one of her cats and fallen down the stairs. I just needed the autopsy to prove it and then this would all be over.

CHAPTER 18

At least I made it home for dinner. They kept me sitting in that room for a good hour before Sue, the woman who seemed to handle all crime scenes in the county, came in to take samples of the cat hair on my pants and shoes. Honestly, I was glad to have some of it taken away. The Benadryl I'd taken earlier had worn off by then and my eyes were all watery and my throat congested.

First thing I did when I got home was throw everything I was wearing in the wash and take a shower.

Second thing I did was sit down at the kitchen table with my grandpa and walk him through my day.

"What were you thinking, Maggie May? Going to someone's house to confront them like that? And going back into that house after you'd already left? You don't just walk into people's houses. What if she'd shot you?"

That had never occurred to me, but he was right. If Janice Fletcher had chosen to do so she would have been within her rights to shoot me dead that second time I went to her house. Wouldn't that have been ironic?

(Yeah, I'm pretty sure that's the Alanis Morissette version of ironic that I just used. In other words, don't line it up too carefully with the dictionary definition.)

I drank my fourth Coke of the day— one I'd put in the freezer until it was almost frozen but not quite, something I wasn't allowed to do often anymore after forgetting three days in a row that I'd done so and having them explode while I was at work. The first two my grandpa had cleaned up. The third one he'd made me clean up. He'd also made me promise to never put a Coke in the freezer again. Fortunately, he'd made an exception that day. Seems there was at least one perk to being questioned by the police.

A Crazy Cat Lady and Canine Crunchies

"I messed up. I know. I'm sorry. But it'll be okay. I know it will."

He raised one eyebrow at me. "Haven't you learned by now, Maggie May? Things don't always work out."

Coming from the man who'd been in prison twice—once for a very justifiable homicide and once for armed robbery—and who'd almost been sent there a third time, his view on things was justified. But what can I say? Life is never perfect and there are always ways in which I wish it were better than it is, but I still believed that things would work out because things really do work out in my world.

Eventually.

🐾 🐾 🐾

The next day at the café was a busy one, so Jamie was stuck in the kitchen all day leaving me and our new assistant to manage the customers.

Honestly, given my skills at customer service I should've been the one doing the cooking, but thanks to the **Baker Valley Gazette** word had spread that I'd been taken in for questioning in the death of Janice Fletcher and everyone who could manage it had come by to poke and prod and figure out why that might be.

Seeing as I didn't really want to admit that I'd seen someone dead at the bottom of a set of stairs and then walked away, I stuck to no comment as much as I possibly could, but man, people in a small town. News travels fast. They knew about five times what the article said and about twice what the police had.

Martin Parks—the owner of the local pizzeria whose wife Gloria had accused me of trying to tempt the men of the town with my free goodies—leaned against the barkery counter pretending to debate between buying canine crunchies and doggie delights.

"I hear you were in Janice Fletcher's house the morning she died. That true?"

Don—Mr. Fancy Slacks who it seemed had decided to make the café his office while he was in town—came over to join us. "I heard you were there when she died."

A Crazy Cat Lady and Canine Crunchies

I glared at him. He didn't even know her. And he wasn't even from around here. What did he care?

"I was not there when Janice Fletcher died." I stepped back for a moment and sneezed into my elbow. "But I did visit her that morning."

Martin pointed to the canine crunchies. "I think I'll try a few of those. So you were there?"

I bagged up the treats and rang him up. "Yeah. I went over, told her I didn't appreciate how she was harassing us, and she basically told me to stick it so I left."

Don leaned on the display case. "I heard there was more to it. Surely if that's all it was the cops wouldn't have taken you in for questioning."

"Well, whoever told you that was wrong. It's a small town. The cops just wanted to be thorough."

"How'd she die anyway?" Martin asked as I handed him his receipt and treat bag.

"I'm not sure I'm supposed to say. But I think it was an accident."

"So it wasn't murder?" Don leaned forward, trying to charm me with those green eyes of his. He was handsome, but he was not my type.

I cleared my throat which had gone all dry and scratchy. Seemed I was still recovering from my exposure to so many cats. Usually my allergies don't hit me that bad but usually I don't have a swarm of cats rubbing themselves against my legs either.

"Excuse me for a second." I grabbed a couple Benadryl and downed them. "Neither of you happen to have a cat, do you?"

They shook their heads.

"You avoided my question." Don smiled at me, but I didn't return the smile.

"I didn't avoid your question. I just chose not to answer it." I looked him up and down. "Why do you care? What are you? A reporter?"

"No. Geez. I was just curious. Sorry to disturb you." He walked away in a huff, but I didn't care. I kind of hoped he'd pack up his things and go. Of course, why should he when he had Jamie's attention. She came out of the kitchen for a quick break and sat down at his table, laughing and talking with him like old friends.

Nothing I could do about it except glare daggers his way every chance I got. Unfortunately, that didn't seem to phase him one bit.

🐾 🐾 🐾

Don's presence made the next few days very interesting in a painful dating show sort of way. He was there every single day for both breakfast and lunch, chatting Jamie up every chance he got. And she soaked it up, loving every single over-the-top compliment and little touch on her hand or her arm or her shoulder.

What made it awkward was that Mason Maxwell had started coming into the café every day for lunch, too. He was more reserved in his attentions. No "you have a smile that lights up a room" compliments, but there was definite interest there. And Jamie made time to sit with him and chat for at least a few minutes every single day, too.

I couldn't figure out which one she liked more. And when I asked her about it she just laughed and asked me why she had to like either one. It was just flirting. A little fun. That's all.

We were sitting out back after we'd closed the café watching Fancy and Lulu play while we drank a beer when she said that.

I narrowed my eyes. "You're not still hung up on Lucas Dean, are you?"

"Honestly, Maggie. I don't bug you about your love life—or lack thereof—don't bug me about mine."

"Oh, you are, aren't you? Jamie. He's a cad. He's...ugh."

I laughed as Lulu grabbed hold of Fancy's tail and Fancy turned to stare at her with a look of confusion on her face like, "Why is this little ball of fur hanging off of me?" Fancy spun around and Lulu went flying through the air, but kept hold of Fancy's tail.

Jamie stood. "You're too quick to judge, you know that? You never give people a second chance. One little mess up and that's it. Done. Over. You have to know by now that no one can meet that kind of standard."

A Crazy Cat Lady and Canine Crunchies

I took another sip of my beer. It was true that I held people to a high standard. But it wasn't **that** high a standard. "I don't think refusing to associate with people who should be in jail for their actions is being too picky."

"Lulu. Enough." Jamie grabbed Lulu and gently disengaged her teeth from Fancy's tail. "Look I have to go. I have a date."

"With who?"

She shook her head.

"Jamie!"

"Don. Happy?"

I shrugged. He wasn't my favorite person, but he was certainly better than Lucas Dean.

Jamie leashed up Lulu and led her to the door, but then turned back to me. "You know, Maggie, some of us actually want to find love and happiness, and we can't wait around for Mr. Perfect to stroll through the door. We have to work with what we have."

I would've argued with her that surely she could wait just a few minutes for better choices than a philandering sweet-talker, an out-of-town busybody, and some uptight lawyer, but I just nodded and took another sip of my beer. "It's your life, Jamie. Live it in a way that makes you happy."

"I will." She slammed the door as she left and I sighed and went to sit on the grass next to Fancy.

"Ah, Fancy. Why does life have to be so annoying all the time, huh?"

We were supposed to move to Creek and then everything would go according to plan. I'd take care of my grandpa, walk Fancy through the woods, the barkery would be a booming success, and Jamie and I would get along perfectly all the time.

I laughed. Yeah, I know. Life doesn't work that way, does it?

CHAPTER 19

Things were still pretty chilly between me and Jamie when Matt and Officer Clark returned the next day.

I was having a late lunch with Greta, laughing at a story she was telling about her sixth or seventh husband who'd been a Spanish bull rider when they walked through the door. Matt led the way with Officer Clark at his shoulder glaring at me like I was going to turn into some crazed psycho at any moment.

"Officers." I stood so they weren't behind me. "How can I help you?"

As I spoke I walked deeper into the barkery drawing them away from Greta. We were friends now but she didn't need to hear all the nasty details of whatever was about to happen.

Fancy poked her head over the edge of her cubby and barked at Matt, standing with her paws on the edge and wagging her tail like a crazy woman. (If she weren't so lazy she could easily jump right out of there, but she never has.)

I looked at him, looked at her, and looked at him again as she continued to bark. Was he really not going to say hi?

He shook his head slightly, but walked over to give Fancy a good ear rubbing. She leaned into his leg and sighed in pleasure. He hadn't been into the café since the day they questioned me so she'd been going through withdrawal. (So had I.)

Officer Clark shook his head in disgust and stepped toward me. "Maggie May Carver, you are under arrest for the murder of Janice Fletcher. Turn around and put your hands behind your back."

"Murder? She fell down the stairs. It was an accident."

"I think we'll believe the coroner on this one. Now turn around."

A Crazy Cat Lady and Canine Crunchies

I started to turn, but Matt stepped between us. "That's not necessary, Ben."

"She's a murderer."

I could see Matt still didn't really believe it. (Thankfully.) "Be that as it may. I'm not going to cuff her. And neither are you."

I glanced at Fancy. "Matt? Can we...? I know I shouldn't ask this, but can I please take Fancy home first?"

Officer Clark glared at him. "She's a murderer, Matt. You shouldn't even be on this case you're so blinded."

Matt glared right back. "Shut up, Ben." He nodded to me. "Sure. Get her leashed up."

I ran to grab my purse and Fancy's leash from the office. Jamie was seated at a table talking with Don, their heads close together. They were even holding hands.

I stopped a few feet away. "Jamie."

"What?" She didn't even look at me.

"The police are here. They're arresting me for Janice Fletcher's murder."

She stood up, staring at me. "What? I thought you said it was an accident. That she wasn't murdered."

"That's what I thought, but seems they have different information now." I was shaking, but I didn't want her to see it. "Can you call Mason Maxwell for me? Please."

She nodded and took my hand. "It's going to be okay, Maggie. I know you didn't do this."

"Thanks."

Matt was waiting for me next to Fancy's cubby. I could see Officer Clark outside.

"Everything okay?"

"Yeah. Ben doesn't appreciate that you should give people the benefit of the doubt."

He waited as I leashed up Fancy. Greta joined us, nodding to Matt. He looked like he wanted to turn her away, but instead he stepped back and let us have a quick moment to talk.

"I know you, Maggie. You are not a killer."

"Thanks, Greta. I appreciate that." Although to be honest, I figured Jamie's assessment that most people were capable of murder in the right circumstances was probably the more accurate one, especially where I was concerned. I mean, I had actually wished for Janice Fletcher's death after all.

"I know a man. He will investigate. He will find the real killer for you."

"Oh, you don't have to do that. I'm sure..." I shook myself. It's so easy to not ask for help even when it's offered, but this time around I really needed any help I could get. "Actually, Greta, I'd really appreciate any help you can give me. Thank you."

She nodded and stepped back as Matt stepped forward. "Let me have your keys."

"What? Why?"

"Because you're still under arrest. I can't just let you drive away in your van. So I'm going to drive you and Fancy home, make sure she's dropped off with your grandpa, and then you and I will walk over to the station. And to make sure you don't overpower me and take off, Ben will follow behind us."

I laughed. "Like I could overpower you."

"Eh. It might be easier than you think. Come on. Don't want to keep him waiting. No telling what he might do."

I leashed up Fancy and we walked towards the door. "You're not going to get in trouble for this, are you?"

"If I do, I do. It's the right thing to do."

I wanted to say more, but then we were outside and the sun was glaring down upon us and Officer Clark was watching us with his hand upon his gun.

I'd never been more scared in my life, but at that point there was only one thing to do. Take the next step and hope it all worked out somehow. At least I knew I was innocent.

🐾 🐾 🐾

As Matt drove my van with Officer Clark trailing along behind us it was clear he didn't want to talk. But I did.

A Crazy Cat Lady and Canine Crunchies

"Matt, you have to know I didn't do this."

He didn't answer, but his grip on the steering wheel tightened until his knuckles turned white.

"If Janice Fletcher really was killed, then someone else had to have been there between the first time I arrived and the second. Did you print the place?"

He glared at me for a second before turning his attention back to the road. "We aren't country bumpkins, Maggie. We know how to do our job."

"I wasn't saying you were. But did you print the cat food cans? Or the plate that was used to feed them?"

"Why would we do that?"

"Because maybe Janice Fletcher died before she could feed those cats. If that's the case, the killer did it instead."

"Why? Why would someone who'd just killed a woman stop long enough to feed her cats?"

"Because they were annoying. The killer might've done it to get the cats to leave them alone. I would've."

I stared out the window as we passed by a lush green field with a worn red barn in the distance. "Did I tell you about the green car? Or the jogger?"

"No. And don't tell me about them now. We'll have to interrogate you again now that you're officially under arrest for the murder."

"You know Mason Maxwell isn't going to let me tell you a thing now."

He banged his hand on the steering wheel. "Why did you have to leave after you found the body, Maggie? Why couldn't you have just called it in?"

"Like that would've helped. You would've just arrested me for murder then instead of now."

"No. I wouldn't have."

"Come on, Matt. Janice Fletcher and I were in the middle of a feud and I just conveniently happen to drop by her house and find her dead body? How could you **not** suspect me of murder?"

"Maggie, if you didn't do this..."

"I didn't."

"If you didn't do this, I don't know how to prove it."

I sank into the seat and crossed my arms. He was right. I'd assumed the autopsy would clear me. That they'd see that she'd tripped and fallen down the stairs and that would be the end of it. But if the autopsy showed murder...

"What did the autopsy show?" I asked. "Why are you so certain she didn't trip and fall down the stairs?"

"I shouldn't tell you that."

"Please. Give me some sort of chance here."

He drove in silence for a long time. It felt like an eternity, but I knew I had to let him come to this on his own.

"Preliminary finding is that she didn't die from falling down the stairs. There was a blow to the side of her head consistent with a cast iron frying pan we found in the kitchen."

"I never set foot in that kitchen. Well, not until after she was dead. I certainly never touched that frying pan."

"According to the fingerprint analysis, no one ever has."

"It was in the sink the second time I was there. Wet." I shivered, suddenly realizing something that hadn't occurred to me before since I'd thought she'd just tripped and fell. "Matt...Whoever the real killer is...They could've been there when I was."

"What do you mean?"

"What if they were still cleaning up when I was there? I heard crashing from the kitchen when I first walked in. What if that was the killer, setting down the frying pan? And when I looked down the stairs, I heard a noise down there, too. I just figured it was a cat. But what if it wasn't? There was that creaking sound on the steps I'd heard earlier. I thought it was a cat, but maybe..."

I shivered, wondering if the whole time I'd been walking through Janice's house looking for her there'd been some killer hiding out trying to decide whether to bash my brains in, too.

"This killer is calculated," I said.

A Crazy Cat Lady and Canine Crunchies

"How so?"

"I came back and they didn't immediately attack me. Nor did they run out the front door. They waited to see what I'd do. I bet if I had called the cops that they would've either run or attacked me and then run. Because otherwise they would've been stuck in that house and caught. It would've ruined their plan with making it look like an accident, but they would've had no choice."

Matt pulled up in front of my grandpa's house. "Maybe."

"Promise me you'll at least consider the possibility that someone else did this?"

He shook his head. "What do you think I've been doing ever since I heard the autopsy results, Maggie? Come on. Ben's not going to wait forever."

🐾 🐾 🐾

I'd hated the fact that Matt hadn't dragged Lucas Dean into the police station in cuffs over the whole Jack Dunner affair, but I was very grateful as we walked up to the house that he

159

was such a decent, caring human being.

"Okay. Come on, Fancy. Let's get you settled."

She followed me out of the van, clearly confused as to what was going on. That's the hard part about having a dog—there are just some things you can't explain to them and some things they can't explain to you.

I dropped Fancy and my purse off inside, gave my grandpa the two-second explanation of what was going on, and turned to leave. But the look in Fancy's eyes as I closed the door followed me all the way to the police station. More than anything, I hoped things would work out so that I could return to her. She, unlike everyone else in my life, really truly needed me.

CHAPTER 20

What followed after I arrived at the police station was five excruciating hours of interrogation. Not from Matt, at least. It was Officer Clark who stood and paced and yelled at me and demanded that I confess that I'd killed Janice Fletcher. That I'd become enraged and hit her in the head with a frying pan and then shoved her down a flight of stairs to try to cover up what I'd done.

He smacked the table. He got in my face. He shouted until his face turned purple and spit went flying from his mouth. But there was nothing to confess to. I hadn't killed her. So as painful as those five hours were, there wasn't much to be said.

Mason Maxwell sat at my side the entire time, repeatedly telling him that I'd been instructed not to answer his questions. If it hadn't been for Mason Maxwell, I would've said who knows what just to make it end. I would've never confessed, but there were a few times I wanted to shout back at Officer Clark that yes, I absolutely was glad that Janice Fletcher was dead. That I didn't like someone who would try to destroy my business, which she had clearly indicated she was going to do, and that even though I hadn't done it I was glad someone had.

I didn't know where Matt was that whole time. I wondered if he was sitting in some room somewhere watching the interrogation on a video feed like they do in **The Closer**, but there was no way to know.

At times I hated him for not being there to protect me, but I knew he'd made the best choice he could. Because he would've been just as hard on me. He would've had to be. It was his job and he was the kind of man to do his job well.

Finally, Mason Maxwell stood up. "Enough. You've held my client in this room for five hours without food. She has rights."

Officer Clark looked like he was going to refuse to let me eat anything, but finally he nodded. "Fine. I'll bring her lunch."

He left the two of us alone. I glanced at Mason Maxwell and he pointed to the little light on the table that indicated they were still recording us. Wasn't Officer Clark oh so clever?

"Thank you," I said. "For sitting through this. I appreciate it."

"You are my client."

"I know. But...I still appreciate it. I...You're a better man than I gave you credit for."

He raised an eyebrow, but didn't say anything else.

As the silence stretched on between us, I asked, "Do you think they'll let me out of here now that they've asked their questions?"

"No. I think you're going to be here at least overnight while they decide whether or not to charge you."

I sat back. Lovely. Just what I wanted was some night in the local lock-up for a crime I hadn't committed.

"Can you check with Greta? Remember, the woman from the barkery? She said she was going to reach out to an investigator she knows. Maybe he'll have come up with something while we were sitting here. And let her know about the green car I saw. And the jogger. Maybe one of those will turn out to be the killer, although..." I shook my head. "I have to think the killer was in the house when I was there the first time. It's too short a time period."

Mason Maxwell pointed to the light again.

"I know. But I'm not telling you anything I wouldn't tell them."

"You and your grandfather. Cut from the same cloth."

"Only in the best ways." I tried to smile, but I was so tired by then. Five hours of some sweaty angry man shouting at you is not exactly my idea of a fun way to spend an afternoon.

Officer Clark returned with a pair of handcuffs. "Mr. Maxwell, you can leave. We'll take the inmate to her cell now. Don't worry. She'll get food." He walked over to me. "Stand and put your hands behind your back."

I could've made some snide remark about him finally getting his chance to handcuff me and how that must make him feel like a real big man, but I didn't. I just stood and put my hands behind my back.

I could smell the stink of him—he was one of those men who get sour as the day goes on—as he stepped close and placed the cuffs on my hands. His ragged breath moistened my ear and I shuddered. He really needed to hit the gym every once in a while if he was going to work himself up that way during an interrogation.

The metal of the cuffs against my skin made me finally realize just how serious this all was. I knew I hadn't killed Janice Fletcher, but at that moment I knew it was going to be almost impossible to prove it. I had a motive. I'd been there both right before and right after. I hadn't reported her death until the cops came for me. I mean, if I were on a jury and someone presented me with that case, I'd probably convict.

And I was so not going to do well in prison. You might think that for a woman it would be better than for a man, but I was pretty sure that little ol' me, who'd never even been in a physical fight but wasn't exactly the type to cower in the face of conflict, wasn't going to do so well. I'd probably be beat up my first week there.

I wondered if they allowed you books in solitary. If so maybe I could just ask to be put in solitary and spend the next decade reading. Put like that it didn't sound so horrible. But I bet they wouldn't let me choose my reading material. I'd probably be stuck with religious pamphlets and books devoid of any sort of nuance or moral ambiguity because some high and mighty morality police somewhere had decided it wasn't good to "incite the convicts".

Ugh.

Which would I choose? Reading horrible awful stories with a message I didn't want to hear? Or not reading for the next ten to twenty years? And what about music? Would they let me listen to music? How was I going to live without music?

Mason Maxwell gripped my shoulders. "Hold it together, Ms. Carver."

"Please, call me Maggie. After sitting here with me for all that time, we've gotta be on a first-name basis. Or at least, you can certainly use my first name."

"And you can use mine, Maggie." He leaned closer and held my gaze. "Do not talk to anyone without me present. Anyone. I will get you released tomorrow. Until then, behave and stay silent."

"Yes, sir."

Officer Clark steered me down the hall to an area with six narrow cells, three on each side. He stopped at the second cell on the left. There was a toilet in the very middle of the far wall, a small sink on the wall to my right, and a large sleeping shelf on the wall to my left that was a little less than chest-high. A four-inch-thick piece of padded material was folded up on the bunk with two folded sheets on top. Must be what qualified as a mattress and sheets in these parts. Joy.

I glanced across the way to the cell opposite mine. A woman I didn't know was leaning against the back wall, glaring at me, her muscular arms crossed. Some other woman was asleep on one of those mats, this one on the floor under the bunk. That explained why the shelf for the main bed was so high. It was the upper bunk.

As Officer Clark pulled the metal gate closed behind me, I tried to see the positive. At least I didn't have a cell mate.

Yet.

But at some point I was going to have to pee and I didn't see how that was going to be possible without that woman watching me. Honestly, the mere thought of having to pee with an audience made me need to pee, which just made it all that much

A Crazy Cat Lady and Canine Crunchies

worse. Have you ever needed to pee and not been able to and then all of a sudden that's all you can think about? That was me.

I swear, in that moment if Janice Fletcher hadn't already been dead, I would've happily taken her out for putting me through that.

I tried to figure out where to go to make myself comfortable, but it's not like the cell was set-up with a desk and chair. I had the sleeping shelf, the floor, or I could lean against the wall and stare back at the scary lady. Knowing my luck I'd end with her as my cellie for my entire prison term and I most definitely did not want to do anything to provoke her. So the shelf it was.

I made up my bed—if you could call it that—and settled in. To think that some people spend decades living like that. To think that my grandpa had. The few comments he'd made about prison had not been good. How had he made it through and turned out such a decent human being after?

(I know. I wasn't even seeing the worst of prison life. I was in my little small town jail holding cell where I knew at least one friendly officer. Ridiculous of me, wasn't it? But when you've never even come close to anything like it, it's a shock to the system. And not a good one.)

Officer Clark brought back a tray and shoved it through the bottom of the barred gate. The "food" was edible, but barely. Think gas-station convenience food. You know, those stale, tasteless cheese sandwiches that come in those little plastic containers and could probably last through a nuclear winter? Ever had one of those? It was like that. Except I couldn't actually tell you what any of it was, just that there was no taste to it and nothing to season it with.

It was like some horrid dystopian future where people live on optimally structured nutrient supplements because they've forgotten the pleasures of a good meal. I choked it down, though. No point in wasting a meal.

(No matter how bad life has gotten, I have never ever taken it out on myself by losing my appetite. Sometimes I wish I were that person.

A Crazy Cat Lady and Canine Crunchies

It would be nice to get something positive out of some of the things I've been through, but that is just not me. I go into "I will not let this defeat me" mode and make sure I'm dead-on with health and nutrition and avoiding self-destructive behaviors. The more I want to drink and do other self-destructive things, the less I do them. I guess that's a good thing.)

After the meal, I hopped up on my shelf, curled into a ball with my back against the wall, and tried to sleep. I figured the less I had to actually be awake, the better.

CHAPTER 21

Turns out that I am not capable of just going to sleep while in a jail cell. I wish I were that cool and collected and confident. I'm not.

Instead I lay there with my eyes closed praying that they wouldn't bring someone else into my cell. And that by the time I had to pee there'd be no one there to watch me, although I could hear people in all the other cells around me.

The **sounds** in a place like that are the worst. Human sounds. There had to be at least a half dozen people there, some of them men, and I could hear them coughing and...other things. (Men are far less shy about the whole peeing in front of others thing. Ugh. Sorry. Too much information.)

A Crazy Cat Lady and Canine Crunchies

Let's just say, I admired that woman asleep across from me. She was made of tougher stuff than I was.

I figure it was about six o'clock or so when I heard a lot of commotion. I sat up on my bunk and watched as all of the other inmates were chained up and led away. Seems the other folks there had been there to make a court appearance and were now heading back to the facilities where they were going to serve their real jail time. So, once the business day at the courthouse was over they were all carted away leaving me all alone in my cell.

In some respects, that was even worse. To be all alone, locked in a cell, with no way out and no idea of who was watching. I kept having these visions of the world ending and my not being able to get out. I want to say **Red Dawn**, the original movie (which I loved when I was younger but did not hold up well for me as an adult) was set in the Colorado mountains? Remember that movie? Russians invade and a bunch of school kids take up guns to fight back? I kept thinking, "What if something like that happens right now? What if I'm trapped here as World War III starts?"

Yeah, I know. Good thing I was only in jail that one night, because I was losing it.

🐾 🐾 🐾

I was tempted to cry as I sat there alone with just the buzz of the fluorescent lights to keep me company. If I'd just listened to Jamie and stayed at the café that day...

If I could just rein in my temper. Wouldn't that be great? To be this nice, kind, forgiving person?

I started to laugh. That was so not me and never would be. I actually like myself, you know. Sharp edges and all. And to be the kind of person who didn't run out to confront a nasty woman like Janice Fletcher just wouldn't suit. As much as my impulses might've led me to this unfortunate moment, they'd served me and those around me far more times than they'd hurt me.

The world needs the Jamies, don't get me wrong. The world absolutely needs some Jamies. But it needs the Maggies, too.

I stared at the far wall and tried to figure out how to get out of there. If it was true that Janice Fletcher had been killed—and why doubt that now—then the only way I was going to get out was to figure out who the real killer was.

So who would want her dead?

It was probably easier to put together a list of who wouldn't. But you could probably eliminate anyone she hadn't angered recently. It seemed to me that most people would act in the moment or they wouldn't act at all.

So who had she been harassing right before her death?

Me.

Well, that didn't help.

I wondered if she had any kids. Maybe they wanted her money. She was from a prominent family, but was she actually rich? Was there anything for anyone to inherit?

Maybe she knew some horrible awful secret about someone and was threatening to expose them.

Maybe she'd had a torrid affair and it had ended badly. (Not likely. But it's not like passion is limited to the young and beautiful.)

I thought about the green car and dismissed it. Same with the jogger. They just wouldn't have had enough time to get to her house, do the deed, clean up, and leave in the time I'd been away.

Whoever had done this was already in that house the first time I was there. They had to be.

Did Janice know? Had she tried to signal me in some way that she was in danger?

I tried to remember if she'd glanced in any direction while I was there, like she was looking towards someone else. Whoever it was, the cats certainly hadn't expected to be fed by them. But maybe...

I wondered how many cats she actually owned. I'd counted...five. But if there were more? What if they'd gone after the intruder and were crying to be fed and that's why the person had been discovered? Maybe they hadn't meant to kill Janice at all.

A Crazy Cat Lady and Canine Crunchies

Maybe they'd been in her house for some other reason.

Had she known about the basement door being open? Had she opened it? Or had the intruder?

I was still thinking it through when Matt walked up to my cell door.

"Ms. Carver." It hurt a little for him to call me that, but I knew why he had to do it.

I hopped down and walked over to him, so glad for a familiar face. "Officer Barnes."

I wanted to lace my fingers in his, but had to remind myself that he was a cop first and my friend second. For all I knew, he was round two of the interrogation—the good cop to Officer Clark's bad cop.

Plus, Mason Maxwell had told me not to speak to anyone without him present. I should've stayed on my bunk staring off into space.

Matt unlocked the cell and stepped aside. "Come on. Let's go."

I stepped out of the cell, but then hesitated. "Where are we going?"

"Aren't you hungry?"

I nodded.

"Well, then."

I still didn't move. "They brought my lunch to my cell."

Matt stepped closer. "Yeah, they did. Are you telling me you really want another meal like that one? Because if you don't, your grandpa brought you dinner."

"Really?" I glanced towards the front of the jailhouse. It would be so good to see him. "And you're going to let me eat it?"

"No. I thought I'd come here, let you out of your cell, tell you your grandpa had brought you dinner and was waiting for you at my desk, and then laugh in your face and lock you back up."

"I just. You know."

"Yes. I'm breaking about half a dozen rules by doing this. Don't tell anyone. Now come on."

I followed him out to the front, the delicious smell of chicken noodle soup guiding my steps the last little way. My grandpa was sitting at Officer Clark's desk, a chair pulled up next to it.

A Crazy Cat Lady and Canine Crunchies

"Grandpa." I ran over and hugged him and he patted me on the arm.

"Now, now. I just saw you a few hours ago. Don't go making such a fuss."

"How's Fancy?" I sat down in the chair while Matt sat at his desk.

"Confused. She's placed herself across the front door so no one can come in or go out without her knowing about it. But she's okay."

"And you remembered to feed her?"

"Yes."

"And to give her her dental chew?"

"Yes."

"And her peanut butter treat?"

He shook his head. "That dog is more spoiled than most people."

"But you did give it to her?"

"Yes. She is fine. Trust me."

"Thank you."

Only once I was certain Fancy was okay did I take a bite of soup. It was so good, but I wished Fancy were there for me to feed her some carrots and noodles and chicken. "So, why are we eating here instead of the interrogation room?" I asked Matt.

"Did you want to eat in there after the day you had?"

"Not really. But I'm still curious."

"Because I wanted to actually talk to you instead of having you clam up because Mason Maxwell told you not to talk to anyone without him around."

"So you were listening to us after Officer Clark left the room?" I tore off a hunk of homemade bread and dunked it in my soup.

"Not live. I went back to the crime scene with Sue. We tried to figure out what we might've missed the first time around based on what you told me."

I felt a small surge of warmth towards him. He believed me. "And?"

"Maggie May," my grandpa interrupted. "You know how I feel about talking business at dinner."

"Grandpa. I think that rule can be waived when someone is in jail." I flashed him my "don't interrupt a cop who's about to tell you something good" look, but he ignored it.

A Crazy Cat Lady and Canine Crunchies

"So, Matt. You have any free time?" he asked.

"I might. Why?"

"I could use another assistant on the t-ball team. I think you'd be good at it."

My grandpa had been the volunteer baseball coach for forty years, but he'd lost a couple of his assistants with the Jack Dunner affair.

Matt nodded. "Yeah, I could do that. Sure."

They spent the rest of the meal talking baseball and the different families in town, while I ate my food. I wanted to interrupt and ask Matt what he'd found when he and Sue went back to the crime scene, but there was never a good opportunity.

When we finished, my grandpa pulled out the Scrabble board.

"Grandpa. We're in jail. We can't be playing Scrabble."

"That's alright," Matt said. "It's just the three of us until midnight unless something unexpected happens."

I was all for anything that let me stay out of that jail cell for a bit, but I had to ask. "Don't you have a murder to work on?"

"Maggie May." My grandpa glared at me.

Matt just laughed. "I need some time to think through what I know. This'll be good. Distract me while my mind's working."

As I pulled seven tiles and lined them up on the tray before me I said, "You know, three minds are better than one..."

My grandpa grunted, but at least he didn't say anything about not talking about it.

Matt didn't answer. He played first and managed to start with a thirty-six point play. This was going to be an ugly game for me. I had nothing. But if it led him to tell me what he'd found out on his second pass of Janice's house...

Well, I guess I could lose one game of Scrabble for that.

As we played out the game—Matt and my grandpa left me in their dust after the first five rounds of play and probably wouldn't have noticed if I disappeared halfway through—Matt told us what he'd found. Sue hadn't thought to fingerprint the cat food cans or plate, so she'd done that. And Matt had found a footprint outside near the basement window well.

"What kind of footprint?"

"Definitely not a boot. Or a tennis shoe, from what I could tell. Sue will match it up to a database she has access to. It has two round sections that are very unusual. Probably a man's shoe. Looked to be a size 9 or 10."

"So the killer could have entered—or exited—through the basement window? Maybe that was the sound I heard when I saw her body in the basement."

"Maybe."

"Were any files disturbed? Did you see any sign of what the killer might have wanted?"

I explained to him my theory that maybe the killer hadn't been there to kill her, but had instead broken in looking for something she had.

Matt laughed. "These days all that stuff happens on computers."

"Well. Anyone look at her laptop? It was a Mac from what I remember. She had it at the barkery the day she claimed her cat was an emotional support animal."

"We have it, but nothing on there so far."

"So we have a few more fingerprints and a shoeprint, but that's it. I'm still pretty much the only person with an immediate motive."

"Yep."

"Great. Just great."

CHAPTER 22

After that we settled into a general conversation about all the horrible things Janice Fletcher had done to people over the years. There were certainly enough people who weren't going to mourn her passing, let me tell you.

My grandpa managed to win at Scrabble, but only by two points. I think both he and Matt were pleased. Not that Matt liked losing, but since he'd only lost because of an unlucky draw of a Z at the very end of the game I think he was satisfied that the only reason he'd lost was due to bad luck.

Matt wanted an immediate rematch but my grandpa begged off, pointing out that Fancy was all alone at home and probably none too happy about it. (Honestly, I think he just wanted to relish the win for a while, but I did appreciate him thinking about Fancy, too.)

After Matt locked the door behind my grandpa he said, "I better take you back to your cell."

The last thing I wanted was to go back there, but I told myself I should be grateful for the couple of hours of freedom he'd given me that he didn't have to.

"Thank you."

He nodded.

"You okay?" I asked.

He shook his head. "People think a small town cop's job is easy, but it's not. Do you know how hard it is to arrest someone you know? To have to think that they might have killed someone?"

"I'm sorry to have put you in this position."

"It's not just you. Last week we got a call about a domestic and when I showed up it was a guy I'd played football with in high school." He shook his head. "He asked me to go easy on him. Said he'd just lost his temper. His girlfriend was hysterical, telling me he'd threatened to kill her. I had to bring him in and lock him up."

"You did the right thing."

"I know. Doesn't make it any easier though."

He let me use a private bathroom before locking me back in my cell. I spent the whole rest of the night staring at the ceiling, not able or willing to sleep.

I thought about Janice Fletcher. And about my grandpa. And Matt. And Fancy. And Jamie.

I swore to myself that if I got out of there I'd control my temper and my curiosity. No more putting myself in positions like this. One night of jail was enough to cure me.

(Haha. I know. That's like telling the sun not to rise each morning. You can do it all you want, but at the end of the day the sun is going to be the sun and I was going to be me.)

Aleksa Baxter

I must've finally dozed off at some point, because I awoke to the sound of someone slapping a tray down on the floor of my cell. "Food."

As I stared at what was probably meant to be eggs, I silently hoped that someone else had been murdered overnight and that the murder would be tied to Janice's and clear my name. Because this was not the life I wanted to be living.

(I know, I know. Not a nice thing to do. But I hadn't killed the woman and didn't deserve to be in jail for doing so and at that point I wasn't sure what else was going to save me. Plus, I figured anyone else who did get killed in connection with her murder would be someone who kind of sort of deserved what they got, you know?)

Fortunately, Mason Maxwell managed to get me out of there first thing after I'd had the joy and privilege to plead not guilty on a charge of voluntary manslaughter. Let me tell you, not something you ever want to have to do, but according to Mason I was lucky that was all they'd charged me with.

A Crazy Cat Lady and Canine Crunchies

Yay?

Mason immediately escorted me back to my grandpa's house. We actually walked there, which shocked me, but as he pointed out it was a gorgeous summer morning and why not enjoy it a bit.

I glanced down at his shoes. "Are those things actually comfortable to walk in?"

"Of course. I wouldn't buy them if they weren't."

I wondered if he'd ever tried wearing tennies. Maybe if he had he'd see how much better those were than some fancy-schmancy dress shoes.

When I opened the front door, Fancy scrambled away. Turns out my grandpa was not kidding when he said she was sleeping across the doorway. She'd literally had her back right up against the door. She went crazy when she saw me, crying and barking her head off.

Man, did she give me a lecture about leaving her alone for the night. But when I sat down for her to climb in my lap and let me pet her, she took one sniff and ran outside.

"Mind if I take a quick shower?" I asked.

Mason and my grandpa eyed one another, neither one happy with the idea of having to make small talk for however long it would take.

"Five minutes. Promise." I decided to just go. Let them sort out what to do with themselves.

"I'll step out and make a call," I heard Mason say as I rounded the corner.

Well, that was one way to handle things. Simply avoid each other. At that point I didn't really care.

🐾 🐾 🐾

The shower probably took me more like seven minutes all told, but that's because I decided to wash my hair, too. I figure that's what Fancy had smelled. It's amazing how much smells can cling to hair and jail smell has its own unique funk I did not need clogging up my nose for the rest of the day.

When I returned from my shower my grandpa had a plateful of

scrambled eggs waiting for me with melted cheese, bacon, and spring onions mixed in. Yum. He'd even fried up a potato for me. **And** put a Coke next to my plate. (He hates the fact that I drink so much Coke, so that was an especially endearing thing for him to do.)

I kissed him on the cheek. "You're the best, you know that."

He batted me away and continued to work on his crossword puzzle.

"You are the best." I started eating as Mason came back in and joined us. Fancy did, too. She never misses a chance at human food, although I had to be careful not to give her any of the onions. Those are bad for dogs.

"So, what now?" I asked Mason.

He studied me as I shoveled another forkful of food in my mouth. I suddenly realized that twisting my hair up in a towel and throwing on my most comfortable lounging pajamas was probably not the most appropriate look. For a second there, I almost set my fork down, straightened my posture, and made sure I had a napkin in my lap.

But then I got over it. Let him think what he wanted. This was my home. I'd eat and look how I wanted to.

He carefully pulled the other chair out from the table and sat down. "Now we set a trial date. There'll be discovery and motions. But that's basically where we are. The case they have is largely circumstantial—no one saw you push her down the stairs or hit her in the head with a frying pan—but it's also pretty convincing."

"What do you think my odds are?"

"I don't like to talk odds."

He sounded like one of those cancer doctors who never want to tell you your odds of making it five years because it'll just be too depressing and, hey, you never know.

"Mason."

"If nothing changes? Probably a ninety percent chance you are going to be convicted. If they offer you a plea deal, you should consider it."

I took a bite of bacon and sighed in pleasure. Salty fat. Just what I'd needed. "If I take a plea deal, I have to say I killed her."

"Yes."

"But I didn't."

He shrugged. "You can take a plea deal and be out in five years. Or you can stick to the truth and serve a twenty-year term. Your choice."

"Or I can find the killer before I go to trial."

My grandpa set his paper down. "Maggie May. You promise me you will not try to find the killer."

"But, Grandpa, that's my only chance of getting out of this."

"No. You promise me."

I ignored them both as I finished up my breakfast and put my plate in the kitchen sink.

"Maggie May..."

"I don't know what to tell you, Grandpa. I am not going to sit here and let a bunch of strangers decide my fate when I can do something about it."

"I did not bail you out so you could go get yourself killed."

Mason set his phone on the table. "For the record, I agree with your grandfather. If there is someone who killed Janice Fletcher running around loose, the last thing you should do is try to find them."

"If? The police said she was hit in the head with a frying pan. The only reason there wouldn't be a killer running around loose is if you think it was me."

"I misspoke. I apologize. Please sit back down."

I sat, crossing my arms and glaring at both of them.

Mason leaned forward. "The best way to address this is by attacking your motive during the trial. There were plenty of other people who wanted Janice Fletcher dead."

"But none of them were seen running away from the crime scene the morning of the crime. I was."

"Nor did anyone else admit to the police that they were there both before and after." He shook his head. "You haven't given me much to work with, Maggie. But I will work with it."

"Fine. Thank you. I should probably get into work."

"I wouldn't do that."

"Why not?"

My grandpa cleared his throat and handed me a copy of the **Baker Valley Gazette**. The headline on the front page read **Bakery Owner Arrested in Murder of Local Icon**.

Local icon? Janice Fletcher? Please.

I scanned the article. He'd really emphasized the fact that I'd just moved to the area from Washington, DC, somehow implying that I'd brought that big city crime with me. You know, like people in DC just walk around murdering one another left and right.

Granted, I'd had a friend who lived in a place in DC where shots were fired on a regular basis to the point that she'd advised me not to walk from the metro to her house. A cabbie had even pointed out bullet holes in the car right ahead of us once while we were parked at a stoplight. But all that aside, DC was not some murder-filled metropolis like the article made it out to be.

And even if it had been, that didn't mean **I** was a murderer.

I threw the paper down in disgust.

My grandpa took it back, stacking it neatly at his elbow. "Give it a day or two. Jamie can handle things."

Mason stood up. "I need to go. Call if anything comes up. And stay out of it. Let the cops do their job."

The cops doing their job is what had landed me in this mess, but I didn't say that. "Thank you for getting me out so quick." I walked him to the door.

"You're welcome. Just try not to do anything that will get you thrown back in before the trial, please."

I smiled and nodded but after I'd closed the door I stuck my tongue out. Who did he think I was? Some rash and uncontrolled criminal who couldn't curb her instincts for mayhem?

Okay. Maybe just a little. Take out the criminal part and it was probably pretty accurate. But if that was the case, telling me not to do anything wasn't going to help. He should've known that.

CHAPTER 23

Two hours later I was going a little stir crazy. I really, really wanted to go talk to that neighbor who'd seen me run from Janice Fletcher's house. Or to Matt. Or to Greta. Or to Greta's investigator. I needed to figure out who had really killed Janice Fletcher. It was my best chance of getting out of this mess. But I knew that if I left the house I'd just be courting trouble.

So instead I built Fancy a staircase.

Yep, you read that right. I built my dog a staircase to make it easier for her to get up on the bed.

She'd been very sad since we'd moved because she couldn't jump high enough to get onto my new bed. In one sense, that was a blessing, because Fancy pretty much takes up the entire queen-size bed, only leaving me about ten inches of space along the very top edge. But I figured I owed it to her. She'd been raised to expect a certain standard of living and she hadn't had it since we'd moved.

So, since I had the free time and my grandpa had the lumber to make it happen, I set out to build her a three-step staircase that would let her just walk right up and onto the bed.

I built it in place, in my room, because the lumber I was using was not light-weight and I wasn't sure the finished product would actually fit through the doorway.

Fancy lay in the hallway watching this desecration of her sacred sleeping place with her head resting on her paws. Usually she sleeps through most of the day, but not this time. She had an eye on me the whole time I worked, silently reproachful.

"This is for you, you know," I told her.

A Crazy Cat Lady and Canine Crunchies

She didn't care. Change is not her thing. And putting in those steps meant moving her bed.

It took me three hours and four failed attempts to get it done. Fortunately I had pre-made risers to work with, so all I had to really do was put boards across them for each step and build a brace so that the stairs could stand alone and not collapse. But that was actually a lot of boards that needed measured and screwed into place.

(I let my grandpa do the cutting. Me and power saws? Not a good mix. I used a jigsaw once. Almost took out my leg. That was all I needed to know about saws.)

The finished product was actually pretty beautiful. The wood I'd used was redwood and it smelled really nice. I was so proud of myself. Until Fancy decided she was having none of it. She put one paw on the first step, slipped just a little bit, and then backed away and refused to go near it.

I tried putting treats on each step, but she wasn't interested. She ate the ones she could reach and then sat down and cried. When I tried putting treats on the bed she sat off to the side away from the steps and stared pitifully until I gave up and retrieved them for her.

So then I spent another hour adding carpet to each of the steps figuring maybe she was just scared that she'd slip.

But no. She still wasn't having it.

Next I added boards behind the gap between steps thinking maybe that's why she was scared. Still no joy.

So after five hours of effort all I had to show was a monstrosity of a staircase at the base of my bed and a dog that now refused to step foot in my room let alone use the stairs I'd built especially for her.

My grandpa stood in the hallway watching me try to lure Fancy onto the stairs, clearly trying not to laugh.

"Don't say it." I gave up and sat on the stairs myself as Fancy sprawled in the hallway.

"What? That that's what you get for building a staircase for a dog?"

I leaned my elbows on my knees and looked at him. "What am I going to do, Grandpa? I don't know how to get out of this."

He sat down next to me and patted my knee. "You're going to take this one day at a time. Worst comes to worst, you'll serve your time, get out, and get on with your life like I did."

I shivered. "It won't come to that. It can't."

"It could. And you have to accept that."

"But I didn't kill her."

He nodded. "I know."

"Do you? Do you believe me?"

"I do. You're a little wild around the edges and you have a temper, that's for sure, but not that kind of temper."

"But then..."

He rubbed the back of his neck. "Maggie, life isn't always fair. We want it to be one way, but sometimes it just isn't. And when it isn't you have to live with the life you're given instead of hoping for the one you don't have."

I guess in some part of my mind I'd thought that this would all just work itself out. The killer would come forward or Matt would find a fingerprint on a plate or something.

But why? Why should that happen? I mean, it was a pretty slim chance that they'd suddenly discover some other murder suspect, wasn't it, when they had me admitting to being there right before and right after the murder?

"Come on." He patted my knee again and stood. "Let's have dinner. And then you and I need some more Scrabble practice. Can't let Matt keep beating you so badly."

I followed him out to the kitchen, Fancy trailing along behind us. "After this I seriously doubt Matt will ever come over here again."

"Oh, he'll be back. Trust me on that one."

I scratched Fancy's head. "Yeah, I guess someone will have to help you look after Fancy when I'm in prison."

He swatted my arm. "Don't talk like that, Maggie. That may be what happens, but it hasn't happened yet. And there's no sense wasting the good moments anticipating the bad."

A Crazy Cat Lady and Canine Crunchies

He was right. Plus, as long as I was free there was a chance I could find the real killer. (I know. Danger, blah, blah, blah. But really? Give me the choice between tracking down one person who'd hit an old lady with a frying pan and shoved her down a flight of stairs and serving prison time? I was probably much safer finding the killer. And if I wasn't, well, other than what it would do to Fancy and my grandpa and Jamie and the barkery, I'd rather go out swinging, you know?)

Anyway. We had a very pleasant evening playing Scrabble—I even almost won a game. But then the next day came and I knew I had to do something more than sit around the house waiting for my trial date.

CHAPTER 24

Jamie and I agreed I shouldn't work at the barkery for a few days. It was going to cost us some money to have our assistants work longer hours, but it was better than people staying away because they didn't want to associate with a murderer.

Of course, I should've remembered the lesson I'd learned working at the dropzone. Every time there was a serious accident that made the news we actually had more people show up wanting to jump. You'd think stories about slamming into the ground at terminal velocity would make people reconsider their dangerous life choices, but nope. It somehow drove them to take that risk themselves.

What can I tell you? People are crazy. Especially skydivers.

A Crazy Cat Lady and Canine Crunchies

Even though I wasn't working I did still go into the barkery to meet Greta and hear what her investigator had found. Fancy was thrilled by the chance to get out of the house for a few hours. The last few days had severely disrupted her routine and she just didn't know what to make of it.

There were a few overflow customers from the café sitting on the barkery side and they all eyed me as I walked in, leaning over to whisper to one another.

(Guilty until proven innocent sounds nice and all, but the reality is that the minute someone is charged with a crime all the people in their world assume they're guilty. At least rational people do. Not like the cops go around charging people with murder all willy-nilly. **I** knew I was innocent, but there was no reason anyone else should believe that.)

Don was leaning against the café counter chatting with Jamie as I let Fancy into her cubby.

"Hey, there." Jamie gave me a quick hug. "How are you holding up?"

"As well as can be expected I guess." I told her about how I'd occupied myself the day before and she laughed.

"I bet she gets used to it eventually."

"I hope so. Or else I'm going to have a very crowded closet. Assuming I can fit that thing in there." I sneezed and reached for my bottle of Benadryl. Maybe I really did have seasonal allergies.

Don had been listening in on our conversation. "You could just take it apart again."

"It took me five hours to build that thing. No way am I taking it apart. I will find a use for those stairs if it's the last thing I do."

You know, it's funny. I say things like that a lot. "If it's the last thing I do." But right then it struck me that if I were sent to prison, that that could really be true.

Ugh.

"So, Don, how's your business going?" I asked, trying to be polite.

A Crazy Cat Lady and Canine Crunchies

"Good. Hoping to wrap up in the next week or so and then maybe Jamie can come visit me in Vegas."

"Wouldn't that be fun, Maggie? You could get by without me for a few days, couldn't you?"

"Absolutely." After all of this Jamie was going to deserve a break. She'd been taking way more of the burden running the café than she deserved.

I sat down with Greta and we exchanged a little small talk. Within a few minutes we were surrounded by the overly curious. One woman hadn't even tried to hide it. She'd just picked up her meal that was half-eaten and moved to the table right behind ours. If the table hadn't been bolted into the floor I'm pretty sure she would've moved it closer. As it was she pushed her chair so far back she almost bumped into me.

"You know," I said. "Fancy hasn't had much of a chance to play the last few days. What do you say to us taking the dogs out back while we talk?"

"Yes. This would be good."

We had a large grassy area out back where the dogs could run around, but because you had to go through the kitchens to get there, it was private. Only Lulu and Fancy were normally allowed back there. But I figured Greta was my friend and Hans was one of the most well-behaved dogs I'd ever met, so why not.

Plus, it would give us privacy from all the obnoxious lookie-loos.

Fancy practically tore my arm off as soon as she realized where we were headed. She loved to run around back there. Only reason I didn't let her spend more time out back was because the border on the far end was just a stream, one that Fancy loved to wade in, and I just knew that if I left her alone out there enough that one day she'd run right across that stream and into the woods behind it.

Hans was his normal restrained self until Greta let him off his leash. Even then he sat and watched her like there was nothing else in the world, not even a large barking black Newfoundland who desperately wanted to play, until Greta snapped a word in German.

Hans immediately turned and ran towards Fancy, all restraint and dignity forgotten as they tumbled and wrestled on the ground. I watched them, ready to jump in and save one or the other, but as rough as they were being with each other it was clearly all play. They were hopelessly covered in grass and dirt within moments, but at least they were having fun.

I laughed and relaxed onto the bench we kept out back. "Dogs are the best, aren't they?"

Greta nodded and sat down next to me, a little more reserved in her posture than I was. "Oh yes. I would trade all of my husbands for one Hans. He obeys. He is loyal. He is kind. He will defend me."

I leaned my head against the wall. "It's too bad when men resemble dogs that it's usually all the other qualities they embody." I glanced towards the store. "At least Jamie seems to have moved on from Lucas Dean."

"Mm. This I would not be so sure of."

I sat up straighter. "Are they still seeing each other?"

"I am not certain, but I believe so, yes. This man, this Don, he is fun and they talk. But I believe your friend is still in love with Mr. Dean."

"Ugh." I grabbed her hand. "Do me a favor. Please. Find her a man who is worthy of her. I am so tired of seeing her fall for these schmucks. She is so much better than that."

Greta patted my hand. "I will try. But what the heart wants, the heart takes. The mind cannot control this. Now. What my investigator found."

As Greta pulled a folder from her bag, Fancy plopped down next to me, panting heavily. Her limit on extreme play is about two minutes.

Hans ran at her, clearly wanting to play more, but with one uttered command from Greta he stopped short and went to lay by her side instead.

I shook my head. "You have amazing control over him."

A Crazy Cat Lady and Canine Crunchies

"He was trained well." She patted his head and then handed me the folder. "This is the list of people Janice Fletcher has argued with in the last two years. There may be more, but this is the list my man found."

I scanned the list of people and their businesses. There had to be at least forty names there, and a few looked awfully familiar. "Give me a minute. I think we need Jamie for this. She knows the people around here better than I do."

I grabbed Jamie and brought her out back. The store was pretty dead and we still had two assistants working for the lunch rush. They could handle things for a few minutes.

I handed her the list and pointed at the third entry down. "The pool hall, wasn't that what was here before us?"

Jamie nodded. "Yeah. And that Apple Café was one block down. I interviewed the woman who ran it when we were thinking about this location because I wanted to know why they failed."

"What did she say?" I'd been trying to wrap up my life in DC so hadn't been as involved in the set-up of things as I would've liked.

"She said that sales were great initially, but over time the locals turned against her."

"Why? Because of Janice Fletcher?"

"She didn't say that specifically, but given what happened with us I do wonder."

Greta pointed to another name on the list. "This one was near here as well. I ate there the first time I visited three years ago."

"Can I borrow your laptop?" I asked her.

"Certainly."

"And Jamie, can you grab one of the Baker Valley brochures for me?"

Every business in town had a stack of free brochures on their counter that listed all the local businesses. It included a map of downtown Bakerstown as well as coupons. What I wanted was the map.

I fired up the laptop as Jamie grabbed the brochure.

"What are you thinking?" she asked as she handed it to me.

"That there's a pattern here. Maybe Janice had a deeper purpose. She was a very wealthy woman after all. And, no offense to you Greta, but some people get or keep their wealth by playing pretty dirty."

I looked up each of the people on the list her detective had made and had Jamie make a mark on the map for each one. Turns out they'd all been small business owners. And, more interesting than that, they'd all had businesses that were clustered in a four-block area of Bakerstown that included our café.

"Well, that solves that mystery. It looks to me like Janice Fletcher was trying to ruin the businesses in this area. But now the question is why." I closed Greta's laptop and gave it back to her.

"I think I may know." Greta dialed someone on her phone and proceeded to have a long, detailed conversation in German. When she hung up she nodded. "Yes, I know."

"And?"

She pointed to an area on the map to the right of the four-block section we'd identified. "This area here, Janice Fletcher owns. And this area here," she pointed to an area on the other side, "she also owns. My husband tells me that the two areas she owns are too small for big development. But if she were to own it all, she could build a big resort. Or condos. So she ruins these businesses in hopes that the owner of the land sells."

"Who owns the land?" I asked.

"Mason Realty. This is why Janice Fletcher cannot just buy the land. They will not sell to her. She is a Baker, yes?"

"So she tries to ruin every business instead in the hopes that they'll eventually declare the land worthless and sell, even if it's to her."

Greta nodded. "And she has succeeded very well, yes? Many businesses have failed because of her. My husband says the Masons are very close to wanting to sell this block of land."

"They are?"

"Yes. He has made an offer himself."

I sat back, stunned. "What happens to us if they sell?"

"If someone can acquire enough land to build a resort, your store would be torn down."

Jamie and I stared at each other. What would we do then? I shoved that thought aside. Right now what mattered was finding Janice Fletcher's killer. I'd worry about the destruction of all my hopes and dreams after I was sure I wasn't going to prison.

"So now we know why Janice Fletcher targeted us. And we know who else might have wanted her dead. But which of them would have done it?"

"There are names we must add to this list." Greta took a pen and in a scrawling script she wrote, Mason Maxwell, Deborah Mason, and Melinda Maxwell at the bottom of the list, her m's looking much more like w's.

"Mason Maxwell?"

"He is the sole male Mason heir under the age of eighty-five. I do not picture his grandfather getting out of his wheelchair to kill Janice Fletcher and throw her down the stairs." She crossed out the names of Deborah and Melinda. "The women are both old as well. They could not do this."

"But...Mason's my lawyer."

"And he's nice," Jamie added.

Greta shrugged. "When money is involved, people are not so nice, yes?"

Just when I was starting to like the guy, too. I looked at Jamie. "What do you think? Could Mason have done something like this?

"No. Don't be ridiculous. It was not him." She stepped away from me. "I should really get back to things."

Before I could say anything more she'd fled back into the café.

I stared at the map. "Mason Maxwell. I mean...It kind of fits. He definitely has a reason not to like Janice Fletcher."

Greta nodded. "One more thing. My husband, he tells me, Mason Realty is no longer considering offers on the property. They are instead looking to buy the land that Janice Fletcher once owned."

"So we're still in danger of being torn down."

"Yes. And...Mason Maxwell has more of a motive than just his business being ruined."

"What?"

"Janice Fletcher would not sell him her properties just like he would not sell her his, but Janice's son does not care about these things."

"He inherited both plots of land? Or at least he will?"

She shook her head. "No. My husband says her nephew, Peter Nielsen, he inherited this plot of land. Her son, Mark Fletcher, he inherited this plot of land." She pointed out each of the plots of land on the map.

"Has the son sold yet?"

"No. I do not believe so. The will was just read today. It was quite the disappointment."

"How so?"

"Ms. Fletcher, she left all of her estate, except for the two plots of land, to her cat, Pookums."

"What?"

"Patsy Blackstone, you know her? She will take care of the cats and live at Ms. Fletcher's home and pay for the expenses from a trust."

"Could someone develop this area with just the one plot of land? Or do they need them both?" If they needed them both then the barkery was still safe.

"They would need both."

"So if I want to protect the barkery, I need to convince Mark Fletcher to sell to me."

Greta nodded. "This would work, yes. But do you have this money?"

"Not yet. But if he'll sell to me, I'll find it."

First, though, I had to figure out if my lawyer was the killer. As far as I could tell, he had as much motive as I did, if not more.

I squeezed Greta's arm. "You're wonderful, you know that? Thank you so much for your help. If you ever need my help, all you have to do is ask." I stood. "Come on, Fancy. We have plans to make."

CHAPTER 25

I called Mason Maxwell and asked him to meet me at my grandpa's house. I figured even if he was a cold-blooded murderer he still wasn't a match for my grandpa and his shotgun. (Which thankfully was no longer kept in his truck, but was still not secured in a gun safe like I would've liked it to be.)

Plus, I needed to get a look at his shoes. If they had two rounded sections on the bottom, then it was quite possible he really was the murderer. And to think he'd seemed so nice and helpful lately. Well, two could play that game.

"I have some meetings this afternoon," he told me. "Can this wait until tomorrow?"

"We're having tacos for dinner, if you'd like to join us," I told him. "I have a good idea who the killer might be. Or at least, why they killed Janice Fletcher."

There was a long pause on the line.

"Jamie's going to be there, too," I added.

"She is?"

"Yeah, she loves Taco Tuesdays."

That was a lie. She'd never been over for Taco Tuesdays, but he didn't have to know that.

"Okay. Can I bring something? What beer does your grandfather drink?"

Beer? Mason Maxwell was going to bring beer? "He's always happy with Coors."

I wasn't, but I was going to have a hard enough time explaining to my grandpa why I'd invited Mason Maxwell to dinner, I didn't need to make it worse by suggesting some microbrew my grandpa would refuse to drink.

As soon as I hung up from Mason Maxwell, I called Jamie. I knew she'd agree to come to dinner because she was my best friend and best friends sit through awkward dinners together.

"Hey. I need you to come over for dinner tonight."

"Maggie. I have plans."

"With Don?"

She didn't answer.

"Don't tell me you have plans with Luke."

"Okay, fine. I won't."

"Well, cancel them. I need your help. I asked Mason Maxwell to come over for dinner."

"Why?"

"Because I need to get a look at his shoes. If he's the killer, I'll know from his shoes. Also, I want to see how he reacts when I tell him about what Janice Fletcher was trying to do and why. I need to know if he already knew."

"Maggie. Call Matt. Tell him what you suspect. Let him deal with this."

"No. I'm doing this myself. Don't you get it? If I don't find the real murderer, I am going to jail. So, please, help me out here?"

"Fine. See you at six."

"Thank you." I'm pretty sure Jamie didn't even hear it, she'd already hung up. That's okay. She was going to be there and that's what really mattered.

🐾 🐾 🐾

When I pulled into the driveway there was a car I didn't recognize parked there. But I soon found out who it belonged to: Lesley Pope. As you might recall she was the very nice former librarian who was "just friends" with my grandpa but who had quite the history with him and probably would have been more than just friends had their circumstances been different. But Lesley was married. To a very nice man who'd given my grandpa a second chance when he got out of prison. A man she still loved dearly even though he was in the final stages of Parkinson's.

"Lesley. How are you?" I was genuinely pleased to see her. After the news that she and my grandpa had a regular lunch date had made the rounds of town there had been a bit of a rough patch. My grandpa wouldn't say much about it, but it seems some of Lesley's husband's family had been less than pleasant about what they saw as a betrayal of her husband.

It would be nice if the world weren't so judgy judgy, but it is. Fortunately, both my grandpa and Lesley also had the love and respect of a lot of people who had stepped up and defended them, so while there might be some lingering resentment and some whispered comments still, most of the nastiness was past.

"I'm doing well." She squeezed my hands. "It sounds like you've hit a bit of a rough patch, though."

"You can say that again. But I think I know why someone killed Janice Fletcher. And I think I even know who it might be."

I sat down at the kitchen table and showed Lesley and my grandpa the map. "See how everyone she targeted was a small business owner in this little section of town? Greta told me the land there is owned by Mason Realty. But the land on either side was owned by Janice. I figure she was trying to drive us all out of business so she could buy the land up cheap."

My grandpa nodded. "Makes sense. And sounds like something Janice would do. But that doesn't explain who would want to kill her for it."

"Mason Maxwell, of course."

My grandpa snorted. "You think Mason Maxwell is the killer."

"I'll know tonight. Matt said they found a footprint at the scene and it was some sort of men's loafer with two circles on the tread. So when Mason Maxwell comes over for dinner, I'll take a peek at his shoes, and then I can know for sure."

"Maggie May. Mason Maxwell is not a killer. And you are not going to go peeking at his shoes while he's over here for...Why is he going to be over here?"

"Oh, I invited him to dinner. And Jamie, too."

"You what?"

"I wanted to see how he reacted to what I'd found out. And I figured inviting him to dinner would make him let his guard down. Plus, I think he likes Jamie. So he'll be all distracted by her and I can make him slip up and tell me something that confirms that he's the killer."

Lesley patted my grandpa's hand. "Let it go, Lou. She needs to feel like she's doing something to clear her name." She turned to me. "Although, for the record, I will tell you the killer is not Mason Maxwell. I have known him since he was little and he is not a murderer. Especially not for money."

"Well, we'll figure that out tonight, won't we? By the way, do either of you know Mark Fletcher?"

I explained to them why I cared and what I was hoping to accomplish.

My grandpa crossed his arms. "Assuming you convince him to sell, what are you going to pay him with, Maggie May?"

"Well...I do still have my 401(k)."

"That's for retirement. You can't go spending that now. You'll have nothing left when you need it."

"I can make it up later."

My grandpa pinched the bridge of his nose. "Maggie May. You don't understand what it's like to get old. You aren't going to have the same energy you do today. You aren't going to be able to work sixteen hour days without batting an eye. And jobs aren't going to be as easy to come by as you get older. You need to save now to survive later. Your generation doesn't have pensions like mine did. And let me tell you, social security is not all it's cracked up to be. That is if it's even around when you get to my age."

I took a deep, deep breath. I knew he hadn't approved of my quitting my good-paying job and opening the barkery. No one had. But I'd done it and now I was too far in to quit. "Grandpa. I hear what you're saying and I appreciate your concern. But I have come too far with the barkery to quit now, so if some ten thousand dollar investment can save us, I'm going to make it. I'm not saying you're wrong. You're probably absolutely right. But I have to do this."

He pushed away from the table. "I better start on dinner seeing as we're going to have a full house."

Lesley patted my arm once more. "And I best get going. From what I hear Mark hasn't done well since his divorce. He'd probably be happy for the money. But you're going to want to get to him before Mason Maxwell does, because there's no family loyalty in that boy. He'll sell to the highest bidder or the quickest cash."

"Thank you, Lesley. It was good to see you."

I hung back and let my grandpa walk her to the door. They stood close, talking softly for a few moments. I didn't want to spy, but I couldn't help it. Love is so complicated sometimes.

CHAPTER 26

It's an interesting thing, preparing to serve dinner to someone you suspect of murder. Fortunately, tacos don't really require a lot of sharp objects. No steak knives, for example. Not that I could really picture Mason Maxwell jumping up from the table, knife in hand, and brandishing it at us while he talked about his evil plan.

One thing I did know—no way was Fancy going to get me out of this if he did do something like that. He intimidated her far too much. But I still had my grandpa. I'd put the odds at ten to one in his favor with pretty much anyone, especially some country club lawyer.

As I helped my grandpa set the dining room table with my grandma's china, he shook his head. "I really wish I'd known earlier that Mason Maxwell was coming to dinner. I would've fixed something other than tacos."

"I don't know. I'm kind of looking forward to seeing how he handles them."

I've never managed to eat a taco in my life without the shell breaking apart at some point and spilling the insides all over my hand. (We're a hard-shell kind of family. None of that tortillas-as-shells in our household.) Me, I just lick the greasy juice off and keep going. Mason Maxwell? Well, I guess we'd see.

I wondered if he'd try to eat them with a fork. How would that even work?

I filled a matching set of red, green, and yellow earthenware condiment bowls with all the fixings for tacos—tomatoes, lettuce, store-bought salsa, shredded cheddar cheese, and, my favorite, sour cream—and placed them on the lazy Susan in the center of the table. My grandpa added a plateful of taco shells and we stepped back to survey our preparations.

A Crazy Cat Lady and Canine Crunchies

(We were eating fancy. Normally we'd just leave everything in its container and serve ourselves up in the kitchen and then plop down on the couch with our TV trays.)

Jamie was the first to arrive. She'd brought Lulu with her and I had to chase Fancy and Lulu into the backyard before they took out the entire living room. We stood at the sliding glass doors and watched them tumble one another.

"I can't believe you think Mason could do something like this," she said.

"Well, he does have motive."

"So do you."

"But he also has the shoes."

She scoffed. "Oh, okay. That's a good reason to think a man's a murderer. Because he doesn't wear shoes you like."

I would've argued further but the doorbell rang. I jumped half out of my skin at the sound. No one ever used the bell, they just knocked. "Well, that's the man of the hour. You want to get the door while I grab the taco meat?"

"Sure."

I grabbed the taco meat from the kitchen while Jamie went for the door. Our version of taco meat is basically ground beef cooked up with one of those packets of seasoning you can buy at the store, but don't knock it, it makes for a yummy meal.

Fancy and Lulu almost bowled me over as they raced through the kitchen to see who had arrived. Fancy immediately skidded to a halt when she saw Mason Maxwell. Lulu, not quite aware that she was facing an "alpha" ran right up to him and jumped on his pressed khakis.

"Down." He firmly sat her on her butt and stared her down for a second until she stopped wriggling. "Good dog."

As soon as Mason Maxwell stood back up, Lulu was up and running again, but she at least avoided him.

"Mr. Maxwell. Welcome," I said.

"Mason, please. Remember after that interrogation that we are on a first-name basis now."

"Right. Of course."

A Crazy Cat Lady and Canine Crunchies

He held up a six-pack of Coors bottles towards my grandpa. "Mr. Carver. I brought some beer to go with those tacos. They smell delicious, by the way."

"Call me Lou. And much appreciated."

My grandpa took the beers while I gestured at the table. "Well, have a seat guys. No sense letting the food get cold."

As they took their seats, Fancy wandered closer to the table, still keeping a wary eye on Mason. I'd put myself opposite him and she happily settled in next to me as my grandpa handed around bottles and sat down himself. Lulu, taking her cue from Fancy, sat down next to her.

"Do you feed Lulu people food?" I asked Jamie.

"No."

Well, that was going to make things interesting. I'd just have to be a little sneakier than usual.

Mason paused for just the slightest second when he realized no one was going to give him a glass to pour his beer into, but then he took a swig straight from the bottle and set it on the table. He and Jamie had a little back and forth over who should serve themselves first and I felt a little stab of guilt that I'd invited this man over under false pretenses. He clearly had a thing for my friend. And as much as I wasn't a huge fan of his uptight manner, he was most definitely a better choice for her than Luke. (Assuming he wasn't a murderer, of course.)

As my grandpa served himself, he said, "There's one rule at this table. We don't talk business over dinner. So whatever business you're here to talk about, you save it for after."

"Yes, sir. Lou, sir."

Mason answered, but I knew that comment was directed at me, not him. I've never been a fan of small talk. Although it did give me a chance to get to know more about Mr. Mason Maxwell under the guise of not talking business.

As Mason served himself, I wondered if he'd ever actually eaten tacos before. But then I chided myself for the unfair thought. Just because the guy was rich and dressed like he spent his days at the country club didn't mean he'd never had an adventure or two. Plus, these days the country club probably served the occasional taco just to mix things up. Small-town Colorado wasn't as small-town as it had once been.

"So, Mason," I said." Do you like to travel? What's the best country you've ever been to?"

As I prepared my own tacos and snuck a bite of taco meat to Fancy while distracting Lulu from noticing, he launched into a story about riding a camel through a mountainous region in Northern Africa all by himself.

"Really? You just rented a camel and rode off into the mountains?"

I'd never thought I'd be jealous of Mason Maxwell, but I was. As a single woman traveling alone I could have never pulled off a stunt like that. I mean, I could've tried, but the odds that it would have ended with the delightful story he told about spending a night in a tent in the middle of the desert with a bunch of nomads and drinking some sort of alcohol he couldn't identify until the wee hours of the morning while they told tall tales to one another were pretty darned slim.

That story started us on a round of telling our most outrageous travel adventures including the time Jamie and I went backpacking in New Zealand and found ourselves stranded on a one-lane road in the middle of nowhere with no cell service and a baby cow that had somehow decided our car was its mother.

The dinner passed quickly. By the end of it I was starting to see what Jamie saw in him. He **did** have a sense of humor. He'd even been arrested a couple times in college. It seems I'd mistaken his professional restraint for his personality.

If I hadn't been worried he was a murderer, it would've been a very good meal indeed. (He even managed the tacos with aplomb. When the juice from the first taco started to slide down his hand he'd simply wiped it off and kept going. He'd only resorted to his fork at the end to clean up the last little bits, just like I had.)

But then the meal ended and I was reminded why I'd asked him to come over.

"You play Scrabble, son?" my grandpa asked.

"Actually, Grandpa. I need to show him something first, if you don't mind."

My grandpa eyed me, but all he said was "Fine. Go ahead."

Jamie and I quickly took the plates and dishes to the kitchen and then laid out the map I'd prepared at the barkery.

"What's this?" Mason asked, leaning forward to study the map, his sharp intelligence on full display as he traced an outline of the impacted area.

"Those are the business locations of all the people Janice Fletcher harassed in the past few years."

Mason sat back. "Huh. I'd never put it together."

"I think she was trying to ruin those businesses so you'd sell your land to her."

"And she almost succeeded, too. Last week the bait shop told us they were closing up. We were ready to wash our hands of the whole area. It's not easy to make a profit when no business can stay open for more than a few months at a time."

"But Greta said you changed your mind after Janice Fletcher died?"

He nodded and pointed to the same areas on the map Greta had. "Janice Fletcher owned both of these plots. If we can buy them from her heirs then the whole area can be developed as a resort."

"What happens to us?" Jamie asked.

At least Mason Maxwell had the grace to look abashed. "Well, building the resort would require tearing down all the buildings in the area."

"So after all that work we put into getting the café set up we'd be out on the streets?"

"I..." He glanced at all of us. "It's not personal."

"To hell it isn't." It was one of the few times I'd seen Jamie genuinely angry. Ever. She stood up and grabbed Lulu's leash. "I've gotta go. See you at work tomorrow, Maggie."

Mason stood, too. "Jamie, wait."

She stormed out, leaving an awkward silence behind her.

"Ice cream anyone?" I asked.

Mason shook his head. "I think I'll get going, too."

He couldn't leave. I hadn't figured out if he was the murderer yet. But I couldn't exactly say that, could I?

He'd already stood and was moving towards the door.

"Wait. One more question."

"What?"

"Can I see your shoes? What brand are they? I have a friend who still lives in DC who I think might like a pair. And you did say the other day that they're comfortable."

He lifted one foot, revealing two rounded circles on the sole and rattled off some Italian-sounding name. "I'll send you the link to their website if you want."

"That'd be great. Thanks."

I closed the door behind him and turned to see my grandpa watching me, not looking the least bit amused. "That man is not a killer, Maggie May."

"He has the right shoes. And a motive."

My grandpa went to sit on the couch, turning the volume on the television high enough to make it clear he wasn't going to discuss this absurdity any longer.

I carefully folded up my map. I knew I should share it with Matt. Tell him what I'd found out about Mason's motive and his shoes. But, honestly, I knew there was no point. Not yet. Matt would no more believe Mason Maxwell was the killer than my grandpa or Jamie did.

I needed more.

But first I had to do what I could to save the barkery. I had to track down Mark Fletcher and convince him to sell his property to me instead of Mason Realty.

CHAPTER 27

According to Lesley Pope, Mark Fletcher spent most of his days hanging out at a bar that was creatively named **The Hole**. And, man, did it fit the description. This was a place for serious drinkers. It wasn't even trendy trashy like some places geared towards the college crowd are. It was just a dump.

It was located on the edge of Bakerstown, down a rutted road that hadn't been repaved in a good decade or two. The building itself looked like an old wood cabin that had been abandoned in the 1800s and left to rot. I wouldn't have been surprised to learn that the original owner had put the place together himself with trees he cut down from the nearby forest.

Aleksa Baxter

It wasn't a place I would've chosen to go. Ever. It was a place for people at the end to drink themselves to death.

But I had worked too hard to get my business off the ground to let one scary, dilapidated building stop me. I mean, really, some of the people in the valley were odd and strange and maybe not good at showers or talking to strangers, but I couldn't bring myself to believe that I was in danger walking into that place.

(What can I say, sometimes when you're used to the big city and the obvious ways it can be dangerous, you fail to see the subtle dangers. As I've since learned, although not in this particular instance, it only takes one bad person for you to be in a heap-load of danger.)

Anyway. I drove out there first thing in the morning as the sun was coming up. They were actually open twenty-four seven, but I figured I could at least wait until seven in the morning to drop by.

I hesitated outside, wondering what I was doing, but it didn't keep me from eventually opening the creaky metal screen door that served as a barrier to the outside world.

I squinted as I stopped just inside the doorway, noting the numerous animal heads on the wall—mostly bucks with big racks, it was that kind of place. There were three men, each seated alone, as well as a female bartender who looked like the toughest person in there. Not mean, per se, just...tough. Her skin was leathery and she was wiry and muscular in a way that said life had sucked everything out of her it could. The tank top she wore had a Harley Davidson symbol on the front and I wouldn't have been surprised to learn that she was the owner of the Harley outside that was about five times her size.

The only real surprise was her lack of tattoos and her bright blue eyes. "Whatchyou want?" she asked.

"I'm looking for Mark Fletcher. I heard he hangs around here."

She looked me up and down. "If you're looking for money, he ain't got any. And he's not the type of man you want to keep in your life."

I stepped closer. "Actually, I had a business deal for him. I was hoping to give him some money."

"Ha. Doubt that." She looked me up and down. "Nice try. You have his kid or something?"

"What? No." I didn't know much about Mark Fletcher other than the woman who'd given birth to him and the place he chose to drink, but I was pretty sure he wasn't my type. "Look. Is he here?" I glanced at the three men, wondering if any of them could be him.

"Nah. But if you want to sit and wait, he'll probably be here soon."

I hesitated. I had his home address in my pocket. I could just drive over there. But maybe this woman could give me information I could use to convince him to sell to me instead of Mason Maxwell.

"Okay. Whatcha got on tap?" It's a bad habit of mine to pick up the accents and vocabulary of people around me. Someone once told me it's a sign of confidence when you do that, a way to build rapport. For me it's just something I do without even thinking about it. Send me to London and I'll be talking loos and mums within the week.

I pulled a barstool out from the end of the bar and wedged myself into the corner. I must've been a gunslinger in a past life, because I always want to sit in the back corner of a room where I have a good sight line on everyone else. Drives me nuts to sit with my back to people.

Turns out my drinking choices were cheap beer number one and its lighter cousin or cheap beer number two and its lighter cousin. No soda. No water. I could also choose whiskey or vodka if I were so inclined.

I chose cheap beer number one, although, honestly, I'm not sure I would've known the difference between the four choices. The bartender handed me a thirty-two-ounce Styrofoam cup, full to the brim. Last time I'd had beer from a big Styrofoam cup had been at some dive bar in New York City that had a bunch of bras hanging from the ceiling. (Never did know the name of the place. A friend of mine's cousin owned it, so I always knew it as "My Cousin's Bar".)

"Cheers." I toasted her and took a sip. (Yes, it was seven in the morning and I was drinking beer, but that kind of beer hardly qualifies.)

She leaned against the bar near me, showing no interest in cleaning the place even though it could've definitely used it. Then again, given the clientele, I figured the dirt and smell of old beer were all part of what made it appealing.

"So, Mark Fletcher comes here a lot?" I asked.

"Daily."

"What's a rich guy like him doing spending his days drinking cheap beer in a place like this? No offense."

"Eh. When people fall, they all fall to the same place. His mom might've been rich. He isn't. He's just a lousy drunk." Left unsaid was the "just like the rest of them".

I wondered what brought a woman to work in a place like this. Did you just over time become more and more of a certain type so that your choices narrowed in on you until you couldn't escape them? Was life just some gigantic funnel and we were all clinging to our place on the sides trying not to fall to the bottom?

(What can I say? Don't give me beer to drink first thing in the morning or you get bad philosophizing.)

The woman leaned closer. "Wait. I know who you are."

"You do?"

"You're the woman who pushed Mark's mother down a flight of stairs, aren't you?"

"No. I'm the woman **accused** of pushing his mother down a flight of stairs. I didn't do it. Wanted to. Even thought about it for a second, but I didn't do it." I took another sip of beer.

She laughed slightly. "Yeah, you and half the town. And Mark. I doubt there was a person that woman met who didn't want to see her dead at the bottom of a flight of stairs."

I sat up straighter. "Do you think Mark could've done it?"

"Mark? No. He's a pathetic wretch. Weighs one-twenty soaking wet. Plus

247

he's a coward. No way he'd hit her in the head with a frying pan and throw her down a flight of stairs."

"You certainly seem to know all the details."

"Coroner's assistant likes to come in here after work. Chatty fellow."

"Ah." I sipped my beer some more. One of the regulars stood up and sauntered our way, clearly intent on saying hello.

"Turn it around, Jim." The bartender pointed him back towards his spot in the far corner. "This lady has no interest in the likes of you."

"No one should drink alone," he slurred, even though he'd just been doing that exact thing.

"She's not alone. We're talking. Girl talk. Go away."

He swayed in place for a second and then turned back towards his table.

"Wow. He got an early start."

"Jim hasn't been sober in at least a decade." She leaned her elbows on the counter. "So what do you want Mark for anyway?"

"He inherited some land when his mom died. I want to see if he'll sell it to me. Mason Maxwell and his family are looking to buy it and if they do they'll probably tear up my store."

"You better move fast."

"Why?"

"Mark's desperate enough he'll sell to the first person who makes an offer."

"I've heard that a few times now. Why's he so desperate for money? Bar tab?"

"Nah. What he owes here is nothing compared to what he owes his bookie."

"There are bookies in the Baker Valley?"

She laughed. "Of course there are. But this one's a Vegas guy. Plays by Vegas rules." She nodded to the clock. "If Mark isn't here by now, he may not be in today. Some days he doesn't muster the energy. Only lives across that lot, but you know how it is."

"Then I guess I'll swing by and see if he's around." I placed a ten dollar bill on the counter even though the early bird special was just a dollar and scrawled my phone number on a napkin. "You see him, you mind giving me a call?"

She took the money. "Sure, I can do that."

"I'm Maggie, by the way."

"Marla."

We shook hands and I left. Call me crazy, but I kind of liked Marla. She was exactly what she was and that's sometimes really refreshing to see. Not that I was going to go back to her fine employer anytime soon. Definitely not my kind of place.

CHAPTER 28

There was a cluster of mobile homes just across the lot that I assumed included Mark Fletcher's home. It was close enough I figured I could just walk it. I'd get there sooner than driving around the block.

There were six mobile homes total scattered in a sloppy half-circle around a dead-end dirt road. The cars and trucks parked around them had to be at least thirty years old if a day, and I would've bet at least half of them were broken-down. The car I walked past to reach the center of the mobile homes had two flat tires and a busted up windshield. The truck parked behind it was rusted through in a half dozen spots and taped up with duct tape in another dozen.

Aleksa Baxter

The sounds of some Sunday morning preacher blared from the mobile home at the far end, but it wasn't the one I was looking for. The one I was looking for was a faded beige mobile home with what had once been white curtains covering the small front window, their edges now brown from years of cigarette smoke.

I glanced around but saw no one. The place was as sad and dying as the bar. Another place people went when they'd slid too far down to come back up.

I should've left right then. I didn't know who else lived there. I didn't know anything about Mark Fletcher other than the name of his mother, the fact that he was a degenerate drunk, and that he had gambling debts.

But I had to get to him before Mason Maxwell did. If he was that desperate for money he wasn't going to hold out for other offers or refuse to sell out of respect for his family feud. I moved towards the metal steps leading up to the front door and froze.

A Crazy Cat Lady and Canine Crunchies

On the ground, right there next to the stairs, was a man's footprint. It had two large circles on the sole. Did it belong to Mark Fletcher? Or had Mason Maxwell already been by?

I knocked on the door but no one answered. Determined, I knocked harder, which set a nearby dog to barking, but still didn't bring an answer. Finally, I knocked a third time and the door popped open. It swung slowly inward to reveal a living room as dingy as the curtains I'd already seen.

(I should note here that some mobile homes are absolutely beautiful inside and my description of Mark Fletcher's should in no way be seen as a general opinion on mobile homes. As a matter of fact we used to live in a very nice double-wide when I was younger that you couldn't have told from a house once you were inside. It's all in how you choose to live under the circumstances you're given. But I digress.)

I was about to grab the door and slam it shut and get out of there, because the place was definitely giving me the creeps, but then I heard a soft moan from the direction of the kitchen. I stepped one foot inside and peered around the door. I couldn't see anyone yet, but what I did see was a pool of blood near the kitchen table.

I should've run. I should've run right back to that bar and called the cops. I mean, I didn't know what had happened there. And my memory of being at Janice's house with a possible killer lurking in the shadows waiting to see what I'd do were still pretty fresh. But clearly the guy was still alive. And the last thing I wanted to do was explain to the cops how I'd heard some guy moaning in his kitchen, seen a pool of blood, and just left. I'd already used up my quota of cold-hearted disinterest, you know?

I took another step into the mobile home and paused, listening for any sound that might indicate I wasn't alone. But the only sound I heard was the soft moaning coming from the kitchen and a loud series of meows from the back of the house. I sneezed as I wondered if Mark had inherited his mother's love for feline companions.

At the edge of the kitchen I saw a bloody footprint with two circles. So Mark wasn't the killer. Or if he was, he wasn't the guy on the floor in the kitchen, moaning.

I pulled my phone out and hit the emergency call option. I figured if there was someone about to attack me then at least they'd get busted for it. Not that I was too keen on dying in a dingy mobile home on the outskirts of Bakerstown, but you know. Only so much control you have over fate.

(I know. You're probably thinking to yourself that if you don't want to die in a dingy mobile home filled with cats in some small town, then you shouldn't go there in the first place. And I'd agree. But I think you probably know by now that I'm not always the brightest about the choices I make.)

I took another step forward. A man was sprawled in the middle of the kitchen floor, his face a bloodied mess. He watched me through eyes that were probably going to swell shut soon and moaned again, waving at me like he wanted me to leave.

But it was too late. The emergency dispatcher answered the phone and I told her where I was and to send an ambulance. The man shook his head and tried to stand, muttering "I'm fine. I'm fine. No need to call..."

I gave him my "are you serious" look. As I hung up, he fell over again. This man was in no shape to do anything other than go to a hospital.

"I'm...fine." He again tried to stand and fell back to the floor.

I shoved the phone back into my purse. "You don't look fine to me. If you don't want to press charges against whoever did this, that's your business. But you need to see a doctor. Because if whoever attacked you hit more than your face you could be in serious trouble right now."

"I'm fine. I just need to clean up. Get a little rest. That's all." He shifted to the side of the fridge and somehow managed to get it open, reaching inside for a can of beer. (Am I the only one that remembers when generic products actually came in white containers with black lettering? Back in the day my grandpa literally drank generic beer that just said BEER on the side of the can. But I digress.)

"Maybe you should hold off on that beer until they've taken a look at you." I knelt down and tried to meet his eyes, but he wasn't quite focusing on anything at that point. I sneezed again and muttered something about cats as he took a long, long sip.

"I'm fine. Call them back. Tell them I'm fine."

"Sorry, but I'm going to leave this one to the professionals if you don't mind. Are you Mark Fletcher?"

He nodded and took another sip.

"Who did this to you? Was it Mason Maxwell?"

He started to laugh but it turned into a racking, hacking cough. "Mason? You think little Maisy boy did this to me?" He grabbed at his chest and winced.

"Well if it wasn't him, who was it?"

Aleksa Baxter

"Friend. We had a misunderstanding. It's all good now." He took another long swig of his beer.

I desperately wanted to ask him about the plot of land, but it seemed a little rude given the circumstances. I would've probably still done it if I'd thought he'd remember the conversation later, but it was pretty clear he was barely holding on.

I sneezed again. I could already feel my throat starting to close up but I didn't have any Benadryl and I doubted he did either.

"Who are you?" he asked. "Why are you here?"

I sat down across from him, careful to avoid the pool of blood on the floor. "Take it you don't read the papers much."

He shook his head. "Sports. That's all."

His head started to droop and I clapped my hands in front of his face.

"What? What?" He stared at me, bleary-eyed.

"Concussion. Can't nod off like that." I glanced around. There was a picture of him with a pretty woman

258

and a brown lab held onto the fridge with a magnet from Niagara Falls. "Who's that?"

"My wife. Or was. Divorced me."

"She get the dog in the divorce, too?"

He nodded. "And the house. And the money. Well, what was left." He tried to laugh, but gasped in pain instead.

I sneezed again. I really, really wanted to leave, but I knew I needed to stay there until the ambulance arrived. Fortunately, I heard them pull up outside just then. Right behind them came a fire truck and two police cars. Talk about overkill. But when not much happens I guess you send out everyone you can.

The cops came in first, weapons drawn. The first one pointed his gun at me. "You. Put your hands on your head."

"I'm the one who called you."

"Hands on your head," he shouted again.

Really? Did I look like I'd just beaten a man to a pulp?

"Hands. On. Your. Head."

"Fine." I put my hands on my head. No point getting shot.

The next few minutes involved me being manhandled out the door, shoved up against a police car, **frisked**, and **handcuffed**. They sure knew how to treat a Good Samaritan. But since I was also someone charged with the murder of the mother of the man who was beat up inside and he wasn't going to be much help in clearing my name, I just went along with it.

Although, by the time they were done I was thinking I should've just listened to Mark Fletcher and let him lie there on the kitchen floor until he felt well enough to crawl back into his bedroom and die. Of course then I would've been the suspect in yet another murder and I still hadn't figured out how to clear my name on the first one.

The officers were deep into a debate about whether to take me in or not when a third police car pulled up and Matt stepped out. I'd never been so happy to see anyone in my entire life.

A Crazy Cat Lady and Canine Crunchies

"Maggie May. What on earth are you doing out here?"

"If I told you I was trying to buy a plot of land from Mark Fletcher would you believe me?"

"Mark Fletcher doesn't own a thing besides this beat-up mobile home and that truck there with the three flat tires."

He removed my cuffs and I rubbed at my wrists as I told him about Mark's inheritance and why I wanted to buy the land. "But when I got here someone had beat him up. Look." I walked him over to the front of the mobile home to show him the footprint I'd seen, but it turns out that when two policemen and two paramedics storm into a small mobile home they pretty much obliterate any evidence. Same with the one inside. Someone had knelt on it. It was just a bloody smudge now.

So I told him about what I'd seen. "And...Listen to this. Last night I confirmed that Mason Maxwell wears that kind of shoe."

Matt crossed his arms and stared me down. "So let me see if I've got this straight. You came here to try to buy a plot of land from Mark Fletcher. You found him beat up in his kitchen. You saw a print that might be the same kind of print we found at Janice Fletcher's house. And, for reasons I'm not quite clear on, you now think it was Mason Maxwell who left those prints. So you now think it was Mason who beat up Mark Fletcher and killed his mother."

"Yes."

"Go home, Maggie."

"But..."

"Go. Home. Let the police do their job."

I shook my head. "Don't you get it? Letting you guys do your job is why I'm now charged with murder. Don't you think I'd love to let you do your job? Don't you think I want nothing more than to hang out at the barkery with Fancy or at home with my grandpa? But you keep arresting the wrong people."

"Well, I'm certainly not going to compound that error by arresting one of the most respected men in this county. Mason Maxwell is not a killer and if I were to even suggest that he was to anyone, anywhere, they would laugh at me. Now, where are you parked?"

I nodded towards the parking lot.

"Allow me to escort you back to your vehicle, Ms. Carver." He took me by the elbow and marched me back to the van. After he'd watched me buckle myself in he leaned close. "Go home, Maggie."

"Only if you promise me you're going to talk to Mark Fletcher about whoever did that to him."

He closed his eyes for a long moment and then looked at me with that piercing gaze of his. "Do you think I'm incompetent?"

"No. I think you're very smart and capable."

"So don't you think that I'm going to ask an assault victim who it was who assaulted him?"

"Well. Yeah. I guess. I just..."

"Enough, Maggie. Go. Home."

Reluctantly, I started the van and drove away.

CHAPTER 29

I knew Matt wanted me to go home. He'd practically ordered me to go home. But I was too wound up for that. What was I going to do? Watch TV? Try to read a book? I mean, Fancy would appreciate it, but other than that, I could see no reason it made sense to go home.

Much better to go into the barkery and take my frustrations out on making some dog biscuits. We were running low on canine crunchies and could probably use another batch of doggie delights, too. And if that wasn't enough to calm me down I'd been working on a few new ideas. Might as well take the time to perfect one.

By the time I pulled up outside the barkery it was the downtime between

A Crazy Cat Lady and Canine Crunchies

the breakfast rush and the lunch rush, so there was just one other vehicle in the parking lot—a sleek black Range Rover with Nevada plates. (Jamie lives just a couple blocks away so she walks to work every day.)

I wondered whose it was, but that mystery was solved when I walked in through the café door and saw Don and Jamie sharing a coffee.

Jamie stood, watching me closely. "Hey. I didn't think you'd be in today."

I glanced down, but there was no blood on my clothes. She must've just known something was wrong. Best friends are good that way.

"Yeah, I know. I wasn't planning on it. But I needed something to occupy my mind for a couple hours." I almost told her about Mason and what he'd done that morning, but decided it was a waste of breath. I already knew what she'd say. Instead I said, "I thought I'd get caught up on some baking. After I have a cinnamon roll and Coke, of course. Or maybe two."

"Of the cinnamon rolls? Or the Cokes?"

"Both." I heated up a cinnamon roll, grabbed a Coke, and came back to join them.

I sneezed. Me and cats, I tell you. I'd thought getting away from that trailer would be enough, but I was clearly wrong. I was also too lazy to go grab a Benadryl right then. I wanted to eat my cinnamon roll first.

Jamie grabbed my arm. "What's up? You seem off."

"I don't want to talk about it. Let's just say I had an interesting morning." I took a bite of yummy gooey cinnamon roll and sighed in pleasure.

"Did you talk to Mark Fletcher? Is he going to sell to you?"

"He's a bit indisposed at the moment. I'm not sure he'll be selling to anyone, anytime soon."

Don leaned forward. "He dead?"

"No. Just beat to a pulp. And I'm pretty sure I know who did it." I stabbed another bite of cinnamon roll before I met Jamie's eyes. "You do, too."

A Crazy Cat Lady and Canine Crunchies

Jamie pressed her lips together and shook her head.

"Jamie, I know you don't think the same things about Mason that I do." I glanced at Don. He didn't need to know all our business, but I had to say what I had to say. "But you have to agree with me on this one. He has the motive. And the shoes."

"Why are you so obsessed with those shoes, Maggie? Don has those shoes, too. He's not a killer."

I froze with a bite of cinnamon roll halfway to my mouth, suddenly realizing what I'd been missing about this whole situation. (If you realized it before me, good on you, but it's not like I walk around suspecting everyone of murder. I should. I certainly do more now than I did before I moved to the mountains.)

I forced myself to finish the bite, careful not to look at Don.

"Something wrong?" he asked, his voice flat and deadly in a way it had never been all these days he'd been hanging around.

"No. Nothing's wrong. It's just been a heckuva couple of weeks, you know." I chugged down the last of my Coke and pushed my plate away even though there was most of a cinnamon roll left. "I think I'm going to go get started on that baking."

Before I could stand, Mason Maxwell walked through the door. He smiled at Jamie with the look of a man who is definitely infatuated. "Any chance you still have some cinnamon rolls left?"

Mason glanced at Don, recognizing his competition, but determined to pretend otherwise.

"Absolutely. Let me get one for you." Jamie took my plate and started towards the kitchen, Mason trailing after her.

"Wait. I can get that," I called after her, but she was already halfway to the kitchen.

Don grabbed my wrist before I could stand. "Why don't you let Jamie do it? I'd like to talk to you about something."

We both knew he had absolutely nothing he wanted to talk to me about. He just didn't want me calling the cops. But I'd said he was calculated. If he could find some way to get me out of there and get rid of me without Jamie or Mason being any the wiser, he'd take that opportunity.

So to protect my friend and my lawyer, I had to play it cool, too. But I didn't have to play it stupid.

"Mason, why don't you join us while Jamie's heating that up for you?" I called.

"Okay. Thanks."

Don glared at me, but I ignored him. "Have you met Don before?"

"No. Can't say I have officially."

I sat back and tried to figure out how to get out of this mess as they exchanged banal comments. There was no way Don was going to let me live, not if he realized I'd figured out he was the killer. Which meant I needed to find a way to alert the authorities. But how?

I reached towards my purse but Don stepped on my foot, hard enough to let me know he knew what I was doing. Okay, that was out.

I glanced towards the kitchen. "You okay in there, Jamie? You need my help?"

"Nope. I've got it." She came back carrying a cinnamon roll and coffee.

Great, now another potential hostage was in Don's reach. And things were about to get much, much worse. Because pulling up outside was a police car. With Matt behind the wheel. I glanced towards Don and saw him slowly ease a gun out from the small of his back and place it on his thigh.

Jamie sat down as Matt walked through the door and glared right at me. "Maggie May, I thought I told you to go home."

This was it. This was my chance. "I was going to go home, but then I decided to come in here and do some baking. But I got sidetracked by cinnamon rolls. Hey, by the way, I don't think you're allowed to come in here any longer unless you have the appropriate footwear. You're going to have to buy a pair of fancy Italian shoes like Mason and Don here or you have to go home."

A Crazy Cat Lady and Canine Crunchies

Matt frowned at me for a split second, but then he realized what I was telling him and forced a laugh as he glanced at the two men's shoes. "That's too bad. I'm more a tennies kind of guy myself."

Mason—who still didn't know what was going on—raised his pant leg to show off his shoe. "Every man should own at least one pair of nice shoes, Matt. Look at that fine stitching. And they're comfortable, too."

"I'll have to think about it. Maybe you can send me a link to the site where I can find those?"

"Absolutely."

Now that Matt knew who the killer was, I needed to create a distraction. I met his eyes and he nodded slightly.

I grabbed Don's coffee, threw it in his face, and screamed "Get down!"

As I hit the floor I saw Mason grab Jamie and take her to the ground, shielding her with his body. There were shots. I couldn't tell you how many. I couldn't even tell you who fired them. I was so jacked up on adrenaline that all I knew was there were shots and that I was on the ground with Mason and Jamie right beside me.

And that Matt was still standing, exposed. In danger.

I rolled to the side and looked towards where I'd seen Matt last, but he wasn't there. I looked down, worried he'd been shot, but then I saw him. He was standing over Don who was slumped in his chair. Matt kicked Don's gun away so that it went spinning across the floor and checked his pulse.

I wanted to stand. I wanted to run to Matt's side and tell him I was so glad he'd understood what I was telling him, and that I had never been happier to see someone alive and well in my entire life. But I just sat there and shook instead.

It was Matt who came to me. He knelt down in front of me and took my face in his hands and asked if I was okay. I nodded, not trusting myself to speak.

"Good. I better call this in."

When he stood it took everything I had left not to call him back to me.

A Crazy Cat Lady and Canine Crunchies

🐾 🐾 🐾

After the police and Mason left, Jamie and I sat out back, still trying to recover from our near-death experience.

"How did you know Don was the killer? Was it really just the shoes?" she asked.

"No. It was the stupid cats, believe it or not."

"What?"

"You know how allergic I am, right?"

"Yeah."

"Well. At Janice's house and at Mark's trailer I kept sneezing because of their cats. Usually if I can get away from a cat I'm fine. But there were a couple times here at the barkery that I started to sneeze or my eyes started to water, too. I didn't think anything of it because the first time was the same day I'd been at Janice Fletcher's. But when it happened today...And when I realized I'd seen that footprint at Mark Fletcher's and that Don wears those kinds of shoes, too, it all came together. I'd never even suspected he was the killer. He was just some out-of-town guy hanging around you, why would he want Janice Fletcher dead?"

"Good question. Why did he want her dead?"

"I'm not positive, but I suspect he was Mark Fletcher's bookie here from Vegas to collect on what he was owed. But Mark Fletcher didn't have anything to pay him. Don killed her so that Mark would inherit. But then Janice Fletcher went and left everything to her cat. I figure Don probably beat Mark up when he realized that's what had happened."

"Huh. Wow. Do you think they'll drop the charges against you now?"

I stared at her. "They better. I mean, Don was the real killer."

"Yeah, but can someone prove that?"

I had nothing to say. **Could** someone prove it? It was so obvious to me. But what if they couldn't? Now that the killer was dead, there was certainly no chance for a confession.

"Seriously, Jamie. Don't say things like that to me." I stared at nothing, hoping and praying that Matt would

A Crazy Cat Lady and Canine Crunchies

be able to convince whoever needed convincing of my innocence.

CHAPTER 30

Fortunately for me, once Mark Fletcher heard that Don was dead, he told the cops all about what had happened. I was right, Don had killed Janice Fletcher to hasten Mark's inheritance. Seems Mark had talked a good talk about how rich his family was to get Don's boss to extend him a very generous line of credit, one that wasn't going to be paid off by the little plot of land he'd inherited. When Don learned that the money had all gone to the cats, he took his frustrations out on Mark. If we hadn't stopped him, the next victim might have been Patsy Blackstone and who knows who else, because the list of people designated as cat caretakers before Mark Fletcher was a very long one indeed.

A Crazy Cat Lady and Canine Crunchies

We learned all of the details at Taco Tuesday that next week.

Matt was there. So was Mason. And Jamie.

I watched Mason and Jamie laughing and talking back and forth and decided that maybe Mason wasn't such a bad choice for my friend after all. He had risked his life for her. Would Lucas Dean have done the same? I think not.

Plus when he looked at her...Well, his eyes just lit up in this amazing way. I actually found myself rooting for him.

(I know. A few days before I'd thought he was a murderer. What can I say? Sometimes when you misjudge a person initially you overcompensate in the opposite direction after you realize your mistake. I know this from the number of people who've gone from thinking of me as a ditzy dumb blonde to thinking of me as a genius. I'm neither. I'm just Maggie May Carver, barkery owner, Miss Fancypants slave, and adequate but not perfect friend and granddaughter.)

As we ate our tacos and laughed and enjoyed ourselves I realized that was the first night I'd felt truly honestly at home. I really had found the place I wanted to be and the people I wanted to be with.

And as I fell asleep that night—wedged into the far corner of the bed because Fancy had finally bothered to try the steps and decided she liked them and was now taking up 95% of the available space—I told myself everything would be okay. I could finally get on with the business of starting my new life in the Baker Valley and spending quality time with my friends, my grandpa, and my dog.

No more dead bodies. No more arrests. Life was just going to be nice and normal from there on out.

Boy was I wrong.

🐾 🐾 🐾

If you enjoyed this book, check out the next in the series, **A Buried Body and Barkery Bites**.

ABOUT THE AUTHOR

When Aleksa Baxter decided to write what she loves it was a no-brainer to write a cozy mystery set in the mountains of Colorado where she grew up and starring a Newfie, Miss Fancypants, that is very much like her own Newfie, in both the good ways and the bad.

🐾 🐾 🐾

You can reach her at aleksabaxterwriter@gmail.com or on her website aleksabaxter.com

Made in the USA
Columbia, SC
14 March 2023

13767802R00171